Saṅt Jñāneśwar

(Alchemy of Emotions)

Saṅt Jñāneśwar

(Alchemy of Emotions)

Raghunandan Trikannad

DIVE IN THE OCEAN OF KNOWLEDGE
Ocean Books

Ocean Books Pvt. Ltd.
ISO 9001:2015 Publishers

Published by
Ocean Books (P) Ltd.
4/19 Asaf Ali Road,
New Delhi-110 002 (INDIA)
e-mail: info@oceanbooks.in

ISBN 978-93-92963-02-5
Saṅt Jñāneśwar
by Shri Raghunandan Trikannad

Edition
2025

Price
₹ 400.00 (Rupees Four Hundred only)

Printed at
R-Tech Offset Printers, Delhi

Key to Transliteration

Vowels and Diphthongs

अ	a	उ	u	ए	e
आ	ā	ऊ	ū	ऐ	ai
इ	i	ऋ	ṛ	ओ	o
ई	ī	ॠ	r	औ	au

Consonants

Gutturals		Palatals		Cerebrals		Dentals	
क	ka	च	ca	ट	ṭa	त	ta
ख	kha	छ	cha	ठ	ṭha	थ	tha
ग	ga	ज	ja	ड	ḍa	द	da
घ	gha	झ	jha	ढ	ḍha	ध	dha
ङ	ṅa	ञ	ña	ण	ṇa	न	na

Labials		Semivowels		Sibilants		Aspirate	
प	pa	य	ya	श	śa	ह	ha
फ	pha	र	ra	ष	ṣa		

ब	ba	ल	la	स	sa	ळ	ḷ
भ	bha	व	va				

Conjunct Characters

क्षा	*kṣa*	ज्ञ	*jña*	
Anusvāra	*Anunāsika*	*Visarga*	*Avagraha*	
Ȯ	ṃ	o¡	ṅ, ṁ	: ḥ

ऽ ' (apostrophe)

Contents

Preface

After a long and bitter winter the horizon blushed, ushering in the onset of spring. It had been nearly three months after which the sun could be seen. The very sight brought about a mood of celebration all around. Under the rays of the sun, the snow started melting and the buds of crocuses raised their yellow heads out of the moist soil. The insects and songbirds broke their silence to fill the atmosphere with music. The change of beauty in Nature continues as before but many, if not most of us, are blind and deaf to notice it. Perhaps presently, humanity is passing through troubled times like never before, ruled by ambition and cut-throat competition; governed by mental involvement and sense indulgence; and afflicted with covert or overt violence. Whether the cause is God-made or man-made is really a hypothetical question. Having lost ease of living, we are being enveloped by disease ('dis-ease'). Our state of mind is stressed and body is full of strain. While most of us brush it aside as a passing state, some of us are worried about the future of generations to come. A question keeps repeating, like the pain of a thorn in the foot: Is it time to take corrective steps? If we are responsible for our problems, then we alone can and will find their solutions.

Paramahaṅsa Śri Ramakrishna was a unique saint to tread diverse paths to enlightenment. He not only experimented but reached the destination of self-realisation through all of them. With his experiential understanding, he declared, '*jato mat tato path*' (as many religions, so many paths). Out of all the paths, he used to strongly recommend the path of *bhakti* as the best for contemporary times of Kali. Many of us think that *bhakti* is discovering our *Iśṭa Devatā* - the chosen deity and getting involved with ritualistic worship, visiting places of pilgrimage and observing vigils and fasts. And we are not really very far from the truth. While *bhakti* does recommend these activities for its practice, they are not its only activities, but something more, much more. As any spiritual practice has a central core without which the practice becomes mechanical, the core of *bhakti* is love – feeling of oneness. Though *bhakti* starts with the *Iśṭa Devatā*, the feeling of oneness does not stop there; it keeps on expanding till one feels as if one has become one with this whole Existence. If we carefully read the biographies of the *bhaktas*, we find this great truth exhibited throughout their lives.

Life of Saṅt Jñāneśwar, also known as Saṅt Jñānadev, and his three saintly siblings – Nivṛttināth, Sopāndev and Muktābāi – known as the holy Quartet of the late 13th century, provides a perfect background to understand and practice this wonderful path of love. Though born in the community of Brahmins, they were ostracised from the society and persecuted. At a tender age, they exhibited indomitable grit, not only to bear the tribulations willingly, but to transform the negative feelings cascaded upon them by the society into divine emotions of compassion and unbound love. We all are blessed with intelligence and enterprise, but what we now need is something more basic – we need to learn the art of regaining the simplicity, faith, forgiveness, compassion and love that live in every heart. This book is an attempt to present the story of such transformation through the events and encounters the Quartet faced with their persecutors, masses and the contemporary seekers and saints.

Saṅt Jñāneśwar's commentary on the *Bhagavad Gītā* is popular as *Jñāneśwari*, and also the work on his spiritual experiences, *Amṛtānubhava*. Though they are extremely important and are works of exquisite literal beauty in Marāṭhi, this book makes only passing references to them.

The technical details of spirituality are beyond the common mass of people who form the majority of our society. A nation's heart throbs with the majority comprising farmers, masons, carpenters, blacksmiths and other trades people. Their understanding about life is simple: they feel the suffering of their fellowmen, as suffering is an integral part of their life; they feel the joy and happiness of sharing the pains and gains with others of their kind. Their greatest qualities are simplicity, hope and trust. Any thought takes the form of a transforming movement when it is caught by this strata of the society. *Vārkari* became one such movement which continues to live and throb even now. This small verbal tribute tries to dwell mostly on the struggle and triumph of the holy Quartet and the contemporary saints, through the *abhaṅgs* of Jñānadev and those of contemporary saints, like Muktābāi, Nāmdev, Janābāi and Gorā Kumbhār. These *abhaṅgs* – small, six to eight-liners, convey so much that if one tries to live the essence of even one, life seems fulfilled. Most of the *abhaṅgs* quoted in this tribute are the ones made popular by the musical legends, like Pandit Bhimsen Joshi, Lata Mangeshkar, Usha Mangeshkar, Sudhir Phadke, Manik Verma, Asha Bhosle, Ramdas Kamat, Suresh Wadkar and others.

Some of us may have hesitation in accepting the miracles that happened in saintly lives, but the real miracles are those with which we come in touch either in person or through their teachings in later periods of time. Aṅgulimāla, a killer-robber transformed himself after meeting the Buddha; Kāpāla Bhairava, a barbarous worshipper of Kapāla, a fearful form of Rudra, transformed into a benign human being serving his victims after meeting Ādi Śaṅkarācārya, to name a few. If we are simple, receptive and sensitive, we too can become a part of such miracles.

Even before the thought of attempting this venture, the author had been influenced by the *abhaṅgs*. His first memory goes back to a blind singer on a ferry, which was taking the passengers of a bus across the River Gangoḷḷi in Dakshina Kannada district of Karnataka, when he was six. Since there are no man-made boundaries of language or region in music, the *abhaṅgs* are as popular in Karnataka as the *kṛtis* of Purandhara Dāsa or Kanaka Dāsa in Maharashtra! During one of his visits to Puṇe, in the late seventies, he had the good fortune to join the *vārkari* pilgrimage to Pandharpur. The simplicity, mutual respect and love among the *vāris* – the fellow pilgrims – the joy and ecstasy in their sharing and singing, left a deep impression on his mind. Later he had an opportunity to visit Āḷandi, the birthplace and centre of activity of the Quartet and sit near the *sañjīvana samādhi* of Jñānadev. That was how the seed of studying the life and works of Saṅt Jñāneśwar was sown. This book is only a humble attempt to share the joy he experienced in the course of that study.

The author's stay with his companion for thirty-one years at Hurda, Rajasthan enriched their life and here they had the opportunity to work for Vivekananda Kendra Vidyalaya. They are grateful to Shri Lakshmi Niwasji Jhunjhunwala, chairman, Ramarpan Educational Society for giving total freedom and encouragement. It is very difficult to come across a person with such simplicity and sensitivity. He has gone through almost all the manuscripts of the books written by the author, given suggestions and also helped in getting them published. Shri Anilji Batra, the general secretary of Ramarpan Educational Society, was instrumental in introducing them to Shri Lakshmi Niwasji and for his unflinching lifelong friendship. He is grateful to Vasantha, his wife, companion, inspiration, support and creative critic.

—Raghunandan Trikannad

A Pilgrim Embarks
(Prologue)

Devavrit got down from the bus he had boarded at Puṇe. It was one of those ordinary days when only a few people reached the town. His eyes beheld the flowing river to his right. The horizon scattered red as it waited for the advent of the sun. Mist rose from the surface of the river to move towards the sky in a warm welcome. Approaching the *ghāt* with devotion in his heart, Devavrit tried to absorb the atmosphere of holiness. The eyes of an old temple priest, ascending the stairs, met those of the youth, who was struck by their joyful recognition and ethereal smile. He was visiting this place – of which he had heard so much – for the first time and yet, Devavrit felt very familiar to the place and its people. He smiled back, happy that he was cordially greeted, but the old man passed him by, without so much as a word! That recognition and smile continued as he approached the water's edge. When he was about to enter it, he heard a gong of the bell and the sound of the conch as if announcing the commencement of the morning *pujā*. After a quick dip in River Iṅdrāyaṇi, Devavrit started ascending the steps of the *ghāt* conscious of the sonorous words, *'Jai Jai Rāma Kṛṣṇa Hari'*. The place was Āḷaṅdi, the birth-place and the field of activity of Saṅt Jñāneśwar and of the *vārkari sampradāya* – the tradition of pilgrims.

Guided by the sound of singing, conch and bells, Devavrit

started walking towards the temple of Siddheśwara, the Lord of Siddhas. Strange as it may seem, had it not been for the recent events in his life, this would have been the most unlikely place for him to be! As a software engineer in a multinational company, he was doing quite well professionally and materially. He was happily ready for the stress and tensions that go along with the jobs with rich packages! But a fortnight back, something made him blow his top to pour his anger out on a kind and elderly colleague, Mr. Sathe, who had made him comfortable in the new setting. Sathe, as was his nature, had taken it sportingly and commented that it showed that Devavrit needed a break! Devavrit, in turn, was disturbed over his own outburst and had walked out of the office! Sathe had followed him to the canteen to join him and asked, looking into the repentant eyes of Devavrit, "I brought coffee for both of us!"

"I'm sorry, Sathe Saheb. I don't know how I could be so rude to you! Forgive me," in a voice choked with emotions, Devavrit said, and with tears in his eyes. He continued after the first sip of coffee, "But tell me, how do you manage to keep your cool during such testing times? I know, it was stupid of me to shout at you."

"Perhaps I have learnt to take things lightly and sometimes humorously! It is said that a villager went to a doctor with a stomachache and was given an intravenous injection! The patient wondered why he was injected in the arm, instead of the stomach! There was some irritation inside you; may be due to your own over-expectations and I happened to be nearby for you to take it out!"

Devavrit had been in this firm for the past three years and it struck him that Sathe Saheb had never lost his temper, nor had there been any case of irritation. On the contrary, he always put the new employees at ease with his appropriate anecdotes and jokes. He was available to all, be it for accommodation, medical help, or even planning a party!

In the conversation that followed, Sathe revealed that he

was a *vārkari* – a pilgrim, which had kept him composed in life. But he said that there used to a time when he too had been quite emotional and sometimes explosive! Sathe had learnt the art of transforming gross emotions into lofty thoughts through *bhakti*. Even as a boy, Sathe had joined his father, a farmer and a *vārkari*, in the pilgrimage started by the *bhakti* tradition and popularised by Saṅt Jñānadev. But of course, he had to be very patient with himself to effect his transformation! He had told Devavrit that the pilgrimage started from Āḷaṅdi and concluded at holy Pandharpur on the banks of Chandrabhāgā, which had another name – Bhīmā. Normally a small group starts from Āḷaṅdi and goes on swelling as it proceeds towards its destination. In this sea of humanity, there are many groups of devotees who continuously keep singing the *abhaṅgs* of saints preceded and concluded by '*Jai Jai Rāmakṛṣṇa Hari*', the *vārkari* refrain. This dialogue and others that followed left an imprint on the mind of Devavrit.

After finishing an assignment, Devavrit had taken the break that Sathe had suggested, to undertake a trip to Āḷaṅdi. As this train of thoughts ended, he reached the temple, abruptly returning to the present moment! He heard the conch and the temple bell in a warm welcome. Light of the camphor *ārati*, waved by the priest, illumined the image of Siddheśwara. His eyes closed spontaneously in veneration on listening to the sonorous voice of the priest chanting the *maṅtras*. Feeling the warmth of the *ārati*, he opened his eyes to meet those of the old priest smiling at him.

Devavrit realised that the smile that started from the eyes had extended to the lips! It was the same old person whom he had seen on the *ghāt* and who now asked, "First time?" Looking at Devavrit nodding in affirmation, he continued, "I will bring you some *prasād*."

Finding a pillar for support, Devavrit sat with his eyes closed. He was glad he had taken that suggestion from Sathe! Devavrit had one quality that he had learnt from his father which had helped him most of the time and that was 'to be receptive whenever visiting a new place or meeting new persons'. It was a while when he felt a tap on his shoulder. As he opened his eyes, he beheld that same benign and smiling face of the priest. There was a peculiar joy in his face, almost contagious, for Devavrit could not help but respond with a warm smile. The priest had a *lāḍu* for him as *prasād.* Devavrit realised he was hungry and gratefully accepted it.

The priest casually enquired, "So, this is the first time that you have come to Āḷandi?"

"Yes! But I feel I have come to this place earlier!"

The priest smiled and said in response, "It was a call from Māvuli.[1] Do you have any place to stay?"

"I will find a lodge."

"Why should you stay in any hotel? I will arrange for your stay."

"Thank you!" responded Devavrit.

The priest just smiled and left.

A little later, a boy approached him and took him to a room.

Devavrit returned to the temple after having his meal. There were only a few people, who were busy cleaning the precincts of the temple. He was beckoned to the temple by the chorus: *'Jai Jai Rāma Kṛṣṇa Hari'*. The same venerable old priest, whose name he had learnt to be Vishnu Śāstri, was sitting, leaning against a pillar. Devavrit joined him silently. He saw a *kīrtanbua*, who sing the glories of God through *abhaṅgs*[2] and narrate stories from the scriptures, while playing an *ektāri* – a single-stringed monotonic instrument and *ciplyā* – wooden cymbals for rhythm. He stood, facing the Lord, singing and keeping time, as he moved in a slow rhythm with so much grace that it appeared as if he was dancing.

'Know him to be a sādhu, a saintly man,
who takes to his bosom the ones who are in distress. Know that God resides in the heart of such a one.
His heart is saturated with gentleness through and through.

1. Jñānadev is addressed by many as Māvuli – mother.
2. Devotional songs, composed by *bhakti* saints of Maharashtra.

He receives as his, those who are forsaken.
He bestows on his servants and maid servants
the same affection he shows to his children.
Tukārām says: 'What need is there to describe him further?
He is the very incarnation of divinity.'[3]

The mood of the *abhaṅg* was so intense that it brought tears in the eyes of Devavrit. He had heard this before, but not like this; somehow it had an altogether different quality. There was a gay abandon, surrender and love – not for anything in particular, but for the entire Existence. When he recovered, he saw Vishnu joining in the chorus: '*Jai Jai Rāmakṛṣṇa Hari*'. Devavrit wondered how the chanting of mere four words could create such an atmosphere of purity and holiness. Purity – as it drove away distractions of the mind, and holiness – as one became aware of the whole and forgot everything else! When it got over, the crowd disbursed and he was left alone with Vishnuji.

He asked: "I do not know how singing and chanting can create such a wonderful feeling; please tell me, what happens."

Vishnu Śāstri looked at him and remaining silent for a while, commented: "You have so many doubts! I wonder whether your education teaches you only to doubt and question."

Devavrit felt embarrassed. Putting him at ease, Vishnu Śāstri continued: "I did not mean to say that the act of questioning is wrong. I meant that even faith and trust should be learnt, for one should dwell more in the joy we get than in questioning it!"

There was a wrinkle on the brow of Devavrit. Vishnu smiled as he knew that this youth was genuinely interested. He asked: "What did you feel when there was chanting?"

"There was a wonderful milieu of holiness around. I felt happy and elevated," Devavrit replied honestly.

---

3. जे का रंज़ले गांज़ले, त्यासी म्हणे जो आपुले, तोचि साधु ओळखावा, देव तेथेंची ज़ाणावा।
मृदु सबाह्य नवनीत, तैसे सज्जनांचे चित्त, ज्यासी अपंगिता नाही, त्यासी धरी जो हृदयी।। १।।
दया करणे जे पुत्रासी, तेची दासा आणि दासी, तुका म्हणे सांगू किती, तोचि भगवंताची मूर्ति।। २।।

"Did you like it?"

"Very much!"

Vishnu laughed and asked once again: "Then why did you kill that feeling by asking? What I mean is that you could have prolonged that joy for some more time. That is what I was hinting at: we easily accept negative emotions and nurture them by dwelling on them. But we doubt and question our positive feelings, like joy! Believe me, you are not alone in this; there are many, if not the most." Getting up, Vishnu told Devavrit: "We shall meet again after the evening *pūjā*."

Devavrit stood up and kept looking at Vishnu's receding figure.

'One, who stands in front of God's house for a while, gets the four emancipations.
Chant Hari through the mouth repeatedly,
the acquired puṇya *has no limit.*
Remaining in the saṁsāra,
let the tongue be active with God's name.
Then all the time the Vedas *and scriptures*
will be standing by your side.
Jñānadev says, having followed this hint of Vyāsa on sādhanā,
The lord of Dwārka (Śri Kṛṣṇa) stood by the Pāṇḍavas.
The four Vedas, *the six* Darśanas *and the eighteen* Purāṇas
sing the praises of Hari.
Just like the butter extracted from the curd,
feel the presence of all-pervasive Lord,
And do not involve the mind
in trivial intellectual debates and arguments to waste time.
Jñānadev says, always remember Hari is Vaikunṭha as
He is seen everywhere and in everything."[4]

---

4. देवाचिये द्वारी उभा क्षणभरी। तेणे मुक्तिचारी साधीयेल्या।। हरी मुखे म्हणा हरी मुखे म्हणा। पुण्याची गणना कोण करी।। असोनि संसार जिव्हे वेगु करी। वेदशास्त्र उभारी बाह्या सदा।। ज्ञानदेवा म्हणे व्यासाचिया खुणा। द्वारकेचा राणा पांडवांघरी।। हरी मुखे म्हणा हरी मुखे म्हणा। पुण्याची...

चहूं वेदीं जांण साहीशास्त्र कारण। अठराही पुराणें हरिसी गाती।। मंथुनी नवनीता तैसे घे अनंता। वायां व्यर्थ कथा सांडी मार्गु।।

Devavrit noticed that everyone was singing, their eyes closed in full devotion. Some of them had tears in their eyes, but mild smiles on their lips! Apparently most of them were villagers – simple, honest and gullible. He wondered...but contained himself in getting into an internal dialogue. Perhaps the words of Vishnu Śāstri still had their effect on his mind! But yes, when he closed his eyes, he could feel that vibration of simplicity, of the sense of belonging to the whole group and of holiness. It continued for nearly half an hour. At the end of the singing, the chorus *'Jai Jai Rāmakṛṣṇa Hari'* started and there was a euphoria of emotions – not of complaint or demand, but of contentment, of brotherhood and of joy!

Devavrit came to, when there was a soft tap on his shoulder. He noted with surprise that he too had tears and there was a kind of swelling in his chest, as if it had expanded. As he opened his eyes and looked towards his right, it was Vishnu Śāstri, smiling with satisfaction and joy. Spontaneously, Devavrit touched the feet of the venerable priest in grateful joy.

Nearly an hour later, they met on the *ghāt* of Indrāyaṇi river. Most of the devotees had retired for the night. They sat on a steps near the water's edge, without exchanging any words. There was silence which was full and flowing like the river near them. Devavrit did enjoy the silence, but gradually when his mind started becoming active, he asked: "What did the group sing, that it created a wonderful feeling of fullness and brotherhood?"

Vishnu Śāstri waited for a while for the question to sink in, then responded: "It was *Haripāṭh* composed by Māvuli. It consists of twenty-seven *abhaṅgs* giving clear instructions to the *bhaktas* about life, this *saṁsāra* and also the easiest method of reaching God in all His glory. It was meant for the practice – and not just intellectual understanding and argument, which are the shadows of intellect!"

एक हरि आत्मा जीवशिव सम। वायां तू दुर्गमा न भाली मन।। ज्ञानदेवा पाठ हरि हा वैकुंठ। भरला घनदाट हरि दिसे।। हरी मुखे म्हणा हरी मुखे म्हणा। पुण्याची...

There was silence as Devavrit contemplated on what he had heard, but not for long! So, he asked: "I understand that he has also written two books and many *abhaṅgs.* He took voluntary *samādhi* at the tender age of twenty-one. He exercises a great influence on the minds of the people. I have read a little on Jñānadev Māvuli, just out of curiosity. Will you please tell me all about him and his wonderful siblings?"

Vishnuji smiled and commented: "If you are asking me out of curiosity even now, then I suggest that you better read more books. But if you sincerely want to benefit from his life and teachings, then mere curiosity will not do. You need to invest your quality time with sincerity and if possible, with *śraddhā* (faith)."

There was finality in his voice that sent a shiver down Devavrit's spine, for he knew that he had trodden into a slippery ground! He spoke with all sincerity: "I must tell you that I have not come to Āḷandi only as a curious tourist, but for learning something that can transform my life. I do have some time and feel that you can help me in my search."

When he looked at Vishnuji, Devavrit found the eyes smiling with compassion and words emerging with deliberation: "Devavrit, all I can do is to talk about Māvuli. More than the listener, the speaker stands to gain. I have always loved to think and talk about Māvuli, and will do so with pleasure."

There was a faraway look in his eyes, as though he was traveling back in time. Devavrit noticed that there was a little sadness in his eyes when he started speaking: "Whatever happens, no matter how great or how petty or how pleasant or how ghastly it is, its effect does dwindle with time. Same was the case with the life and teachings of Māvuli. The persons, who were transformed because of this great saint, lived their life and passed away. As it always happens, their experiences turned into memories of those with whom they had shared, to, in turn, become stories. Gradually even these stories faded from the speech and minds of the people. Nearly two hundred years had to elapse after the passing of Jñānadev Māvuli before the advent of one more saint. Providence had chosen him to revive whatever Māvuli had taught. He did just that by living that very Truth."

The fourth-day moon of the dark fortnight had risen. Looking at it, Vishnuji joined his palms in veneration. In the mild pleasant breeze, the leaves on the trees above made a whispering sound. They appeared to say to Devavrit, 'Listen... listen with your heart!' As if joining them, Vishnuji said with a smile: "All of us, without any exception, feel that the life of *bhaktas* is quite easy, while ours is tough! All our problems are insurmountable, while that of others are petty! If you ask me, I say, that only those, who prove their mettle in facing their problems, in taking every opportunity to solve those of others, are called as *bhaktas*. They just appear on this planet, live their lives naturally, without even being conscious of their being *bhaktas*!"

River Iṅdrāyaṇi joined him with her steady gurgle. At the far end of the flow, the trees cast their shadows. The town appeared to have gone into the laps of sleep.

"Like the *saṅgam*, the confluence, of the Gaṅgā, Yamunā and Saraswatī, Māvuli's life has the *saṅgam* of three saints: one of spiritual River Gaṅgā of Māvuli consisting of four tributaries of Nivṛttināth Mahārāj, Jñāneśwar Mahārāj, Sopāndev and Muktāyī, Yamunā of Saṅt Nāmdev Mahārāj, Saṅt Janābāī and Saṅt Gorobā Kumbhār, and Saraswatī of Saṅt Ekanāth Mahārāj. Times were indeed troubled, with invasion from outside our land and from within. Providence had chosen them and other *bhaktas* to wipe the tears of the suffering lot through their own tears – tears for their chosen God and to give direction to the society."

And thus Vishnuji started his grand narration...

1
The Dream

The moon was moving towards the western horizon, while dawn made the announcement of the arrival of a new day ahead, of new experiences, of new acquaintances and may be friends. Ekanāth, who had just completed five years in this world, was hurrying towards the river. Orphaned while he was just an infant, he had been brought up by his grandfather Bhānudās, a saint of *vārkari* tradition, with much difficulty. Knowing that his days were numbered, he had ascertained that Ekanāth grew up on his own. Even as a toddler, he had taken him to the river to introduce her as his eternal mother. Trusting, as most children are, he had believed her to be so.

Only the previous day, Bhānudāsji had managed to conduct his *yajñopavit* ceremony. Ekanāth wanted to show his new ornament, the *yajñopavit* – the sacred thread, to his mother. When he saw the speeding waters making a gurgling sound, he felt her joy beckoning him towards her and he ran to the water's edge and dived in. Mother enveloped the son, taking him into her arms and blessed him, who had become a *brahmacāri* the day before! The river was Godāvari and the place was Paiṭhan.

The peers of his age, tied to their parent's apron strings, were scared to go near the water. But not Ekanāth, for how could he possibly be scared of his mother? In spite of the concern shown by the town's people, his grandfather had allowed him to be totally free with the river. Godāmāyī, as he addressed her, had been his first teacher as most mothers are. After the fun and frolic in her waters, Ekyā (as he was fondly addressed by his grandfather and others) would sit on the step nearest to the water and keep looking and listening to her. In her continual movement, he saw her graceful gestures and in her flowing sounds, sometimes in whispers, other times, soft and musical and yet other times, loud and threatening – he could listen to the words of love, of compassion and even admonition! He noticed that her incessant flow was teaching him to flow with time and circumstances. She allowed everyone to enter her without any resistance as she accepted everyone as she or he was! Whoever entered her was refreshed and purified without any discrimination whatsoever. Perhaps his intimacy with the river made him imbibe the very qualities from her. Ekanāth's first *guru* was River Godāvari.

Ekanāth felt that Godāmāyī directed him to search for his *guru* in human form and to proceed to Daulatābād fort. He took the permission of his grandfather Bhānudās to leave Paiṭhan. He was blessed at the meeting with Janardhan Swami. Unlike many traditional spiritual masters, Janardhan Swami was not a *sannyasi* in clothes, but was the *guru* of many *sannyasins*. Janardhan Swami was in-charge of the fort, appointed by the Muslim king! Ekanāth saw that his master changed his role from a spiritual master to an able administrator very easily. He could be a taskmaster when he allotted certain daily chores and was equally, if not stricter, when it came to matters spiritual.

Once Ekanāth spent a whole night trying to find an accounting mistake of one pie (the coin of smallest denomination)! Janardhan Swamiji just patted him on his shoulder and observed that he should show the same sincerity to search for the Divine. Janardhan Swami had followers and disciples from all castes and also Muslims. He guided all of them without any discrimination, but with equal zest and sincerity. Anybody could approach him for solutions to not only their spiritual doubts, but also worldly problems. Just by being with him, they were at peace. Ekyā noted his *guru* had fluid nature, acceptance as well as benevolence. He gratefully remembered his Godāmāyī!

Janardhan Swamiji, in turn, found Ekyā to be a very receptive, thirsty for knowing (as different from 'knowledge') and a ready learner. He taught Ekanāth the *Vedānta*, *nyāya*, *mīmānsa* (reflection), *yoga,* etc. and most importantly, Sant Jñānadev's works. Janardhan Swami had the manuscripts of the saint. Ekanāth was fascinated by the broad-mindedness and all-inclusiveness of his teachings which accepted every being's right to realise the Truth. He discovered that the scriptures explained the same Truth from different perspectives and languages. When he approached his *guru* and shared this insight, he could see that twinkle of satisfaction in his eyes, but there was seriousness on his countenance.

Janardhan Swami observed: "Ekyā, you have crossed the easy part of your search. Now you will have to start on the more challenging task." Noting the expression of his disciple, he continued: "Let me ask you, as to why you have come here?"

Ekyā responded: "To learn and..."

There was hesitation, so Swami goaded him towards the truth: "And...don't hesitate; complete your thoughts!"

After a while, Ekyā said: "And to experience the Divine!"

Swami laughed in all joy and remarked: "To experience and to be one with the Divine! You have understood the spirit of our scriptures intellectually. Now you have to start living that spirit."

Spontaneously, Ekyā fell prostrate at the lotus feet of his master. In that one small gesture of his, there was total trust, reception and surrender. The master rose to embrace him. There were tears in both of them's eyes – that of joy in the master and on receiving the grace, in the disciple. Putting a palm on the shoulder of Ekyā, Swami said: "Now it is time for you to live in solitude."

Ekyā, in turn, asked with a tone of concern: "But what about your guidance?"

Smiling benevolently, the master replied: "You have Jñāneśwar Māvulī with you, what more do you want?"

And so, Ekanāth left the *gurukul* to walk towards the wilderness that was beckoning him to receive what it had to offer. After the passage of some time, Ekanāth had apparently lived under the direction of *bhāvartha deepika (Jñāneśwari)* and *Amṛtānubhava*. But mostly in his lonely moments, he would hum the *abhaṅgs* that gave him courage and grit to continue.

And one day, unasked, un-thought and quite unexpectedly, he saw the form of Kṛṣṇa *ghanaśyāma* (of the colour of the dark rain-bearing cloud). He was happy, nay joyous, nay ecstatic and lost consciousness of the outer world. This was his first experience and definitely not the last! He had to share it with his master!

Janardhan Swami, who was busy amidst his administrative affairs, saw the form of Ekyā approaching him in all eagerness, but he continued with his engagement, without as much as giving a second look! Ekyā waited for his master, who noticed inconspicuously that Ekyā was not even aware, that he was waiting! Much later, Swamiji left for his bath, ritualistic worship of his *Iśṭa,* the chosen deity Dattātreya; then for his lunch and afternoon nap! Ekyā remained sitting on the same spot, waiting for the arrival of his master!

It was early evening, when Janardhan Swami came to the spot and found Ekyā sitting with his eyes closed. There was an ethereal glow on his countenance. Swamiji called with all affection: "Ekyā!" In response to which, Ekanāth got up and fell prostrate at the feet of his master, who continued: "So, you have seen Him?! Good, but not enough.

Ekanāth got up and whispered: "In which case, I will return to the wilderness!"

"That is not what I meant. You must return to Paiṭhan and step into *gṛhastāśrama*. Live the so-called ordinary life, with your feet firmly on the ground, but your spirit soaring up in the skies!"

Ekanāth started his journey back to Paiṭhan very next morning, after taking leave of his beloved master. He was calm and composed for he carried with him manuscripts of Māvulī, and also the blessings of his master! It was noon and the sun was at his zenith. Noticing a shady tree, Ekanāth decided to rest for a while. Nearby, there was a small meandering stream. After washing his feet and face, he leaned against the tree. As soon as he closed his eyes, he remembered that wonderful form of Kṛṣṇa Ghanaśyāma (the colour of dark rain-bearing cloud). There was so much feeling that an *abhaṅg* rushed out of his being:

> '*How did you forsake me,* O Rāma?
> *Without Rāma, the soul is agitated, not knowing what to do.*
> *Without Rāma, neither is any peace for me, nor any rest for my soul.*
> *Let Ekā of Janardhan behold your form again with these eyes, O Ghanaśyāma.*'[5]

A few parrots that were perched on the tree, joined in, as if responding to his call to the Divine! There were tears of joy, his hair stood on end and his chest blushed with sheer pleasure. For him, Nature stood still. By the time he came to, he realised that it was early evening as he beheld the sun slowly approaching the horizon. But his mind was still like a wave-less lake reflecting the sky, while showing the lake-bed in all clarity! He realised that he had merged with Nature around; nay, it had enveloped him under its embrace! Ghanaśyāma was the cloud reflecting the gold of the sun, while the sun, in turn, illuminated the world...every being and everything had become Divine. A great insight dawned on him, never to leave his being: In the infinite Divine Ocean, each one of us is a wave frolicking in it, eternally with it!

---

5. कसा मला टाकुन गेला राम। रामा वीण जीव व्याकुळ होतो, सुचत नाही काम।।
रामा वीण मज्ञ चैन पडेना, नाही जिवासी आराम।
एका जनार्दनी पाहुनि डोळ्या, रुप तुज्ञे घनश्याम।।

When he returned to Paiṭhan, his grandparents were overjoyed. Bhānudās recognised his enlightened grandson! When they both directed him to take to *gṛhastāśrama*, he readily agreed and was married to Girijā, who made an ideal companion for leading an exemplary ethical life. In due course, they were blessed with two daughters, Godāvari and Gaṅgā and a son, Hari. There were many occasions when their grit and patience were tested to the limit.

It was dawn and the town of Paiṭhan was astir with activity. The cowherds and shepherds were on their way to the grazing grounds. The temple priests were approaching Godāvari for their bath. As they were about to start descending the steps of the *ghāt,* they were astonished by what they saw: standing in chest-deep water, Ekanāth was trying to save a scorpion from drowning! When he was about to throw it on to the ground, it stung his finger. Due to the intense pain, his palms opened and the scorpion fell into the water. Ekanāth picked up the insect once again and was again stung by it! This continued five times and the sixth time, he succeeded in saving it. After finishing his bath, he started climbing the steps, when one of the priests commented in sarcasm: "We suspected that you are mad, but today you have proved it!"

Ekanāth asked innocently: "Why do you say that?"

All the persons who had seen what had happened laughed aloud. "The very first time, you learnt that the scorpion stings you if you even touch it. Why did you insist on saving it?"

Ekanāth smiled and responded: "If the scorpion, an insect, is adamant not to digress from its *dharma*, why should I do so?" Noting that they had not understood what he was hinting at, he continued: "Stinging is the *dharma* of the scorpion. I am supposed to be a Brāhmaṇa whose *dharma* is to be compassionate, kind and protective. Why should I digress from mine?"

As if in agreement, a cool mild breeze started blowing, bringing respite to the hot and humid climate.

One day he saw a child, who had just started walking,

crying as he was alone and walking on a rock. It was noon and the sun was at its zenith, making his feet burn. Many persons passing by did not even notice the child, for he was from a lower caste and considered untouchable! When Ekanāth saw him, he immediately rushed to him and hugged the child to his bosom. Seeing this, the Brahmins showed their anger and questioned him.

Quoting *Srīmad Bhagavad Gītā*[6], he told them that the castes were created by the Lord according to their nature and actions. A real Brāhmaṇa is compassionate and it is not enough to learn scriptures by rote, but we should live the principles therein.

The benediction of Janardhan Swami, well known for his broad-mindedness and all-encompassing nature, and the infinite patience of Jñānadev, had a great influence over him. Both these saints had so touched his being that he had become extremely patient, understanding and tolerant. Actually it could not be even called tolerance; it was total acceptance of the whole universe as it is. This nobility was successfully transferred by him to his entire family.

But, as it always happens in the world, this great quality was misunderstood as foolishness or gullibility! Many people, who came in touch with him, took advantage of his large-heartedness. Whenever there is some extraordinary quality in someone, it is either despised or worshipped, but can never be ignored! Initially such persons are always seen with suspicion or even malice! Then a few gather around him, like bees get attracted to honey, when he adheres steadfastly to his ideals and his nature. If there is goodness, it spreads. When asked as to how he could be calm and patient under all circumstances, he would remark with a smile: "When you are convinced that God is always with you, looking after you and nurturing you, you start imbibing His qualities. Let me narrate an anecdote of Śri Viṣṇu. Sage Bhṛgu wanted to have a consultation with Lord Brahmā. When he reached *satyaloka*, he found the God busy

---

6. चातुर्वर्ण्यं मया सृष्टं गुणकर्मविभागशः। तस्य कर्तारमपि मां विद्ध्यकर्तारमव्ययम्।। श्रीमद्भगवद्गीता ४.१३।।

chanting the *Vedas* with Goddess Saraswatī. The sage was not happy but he proceeded to Mount Kailās, the abode of Mahādev, the great God Śiva, who, in turn, was in deep communion with Goddess Pārvati because of which they did not even notice the arrival of the sage. This annoyed him to the point of irritation! He felt he should proceed to Vaikunṭha, the abode of Viṣṇu. Nārāyaṇa was at rest, with Goddess Lakṣmi massaging his feet. By that time, Sage Bhṛgu lost all patience and rushed to the bed of Snake Anaṅta and kicked the Lord in the chest! The Lord got up and rushed to the sage and massaged his feet! The Lord asked apologetically: "Did it hurt you?"

The sage was pacified and left after the consultation. The goddess was angry at the behaviour of the sage and with Lord's response. She asked: "How could you be so patient with the outrageous act of Bhṛgu?"

The Lord replied smilingly: "Will you get angry with your child for kicking your chest when he tries to climb on your shoulders? This whole Existence is not only our creation but '*I*'. How can I be impatient with self?"

Ekanāth's legendary patience brought him the title *Śāṅtibrahma*, the 'Peaceful Brahman'. He was at peace with himself as well as the world.

Once, when he was asked by someone about his not going on a pilgrimage to Pandharpur, he sang in response:

'My body is Panḍhari, and my soul is Viṭṭhala
Pānḍuraṅga alone rules my being.
Emotions and devotion in Pānḍuraṅga, are the flowing waters of Bhīmā river.
Compassion, forgiveness, and peace within is like
Gathering of Vaiśṇavas in the sands of Caṅdrabhāga (Bhīma river).
Awareness of God, meditation, prayer and bliss through discrimination
Is like the divine notes from Kṛṣṇa's flute.
My offering to God is the act of gathering of all my ten organs.

Ekā of Janardhan says that he sees sanctity of Paṇḍhari
in self, in people and in Nature.
And the real place of pilgrimage is within.[7]

Ekanāth had said it all! There was nothing to seek and nowhere to go! But was it really so? Even the enlightened have not finished their mission until it is time for them to shed their bodies.

It was the sixth day of the *Kṛṣṇa Pakṣa*, the dark fortnight of the month of *Phālguna*. Every household in the town of Paiṭhan was silently resting in the laps of sleep, but strange as it may seem, Ekanāth was unable to sleep. He had this rising feeling that something had been left undone, a feeling of incompleteness.

In the early hours of the morning, he fell into deep sleep as his mind came to rest. He heard someone call: "Ekanāth!!" When he responded through his attention, he saw a youth, radiant and fresh, sitting in the meditative posture. Near the left knee fluttered the pages of a manuscript. To his surprise, he found that the roots of a tree had enveloped and strangled the neck of that youth and there was concern on that face. Ekanāth prostrated and stood in waiting to receive whatever the youth had to give. The voice, sweet but commanding at the same time, said: "Ekanāth, you must come here and free me from the strangulation of the roots of *Ajāna* tree. Do not waste any time; reach as soon as possible. I have an important work for you."

Soon Ekanāth heard a cock crow. He woke up. There was a peculiar alertness that made him ask questions, 'Who was it?' It was definitely not *guruji*, for he had addressed him always as Ekyā! It suddenly dawned on him that it was Jñānadev

---

7. काया ही पंढरी आत्म हा विट्ठल। नांदतो केवळ पांडुरंग।।
भाव भक्ति भीमा उदक ते वाहे, बरवा शोभताहे पांडुरंग।। १।।
दया क्षमा शांति हेंचि वाळावंट, मिळालासे थाट वैष्णवांचा।। २।।
ज्ञान ध्यान पूजा विवेक आनंद, हाचि वेणुनाद शोभतसे।। ३।।
दश इंद्रियांचा एक मेळा केला, ऐसा गोपाळकाला होत असे।। ४।।
देखिली पंढरी देही जनी वनी, एका जनार्दनी वारी करी।। ५।।

Māvuli. He was enthused and proceeded to *Godāmāyi* where he found a few companions. Narrating his dream, he told them of his decision to proceed to Āḷaṅdi. After taking leave of his devout wife Girijā and daughters, they started their pilgrimage to Āḷandi. The orthodox felt that he was going in the wrong direction for the pilgrimage that started from Āḷaṅdi and concluded at Pandharpur! Ekanāth responded by saying that he was on a pilgrimage to the root!

The two companions, son Hari and friend Balavant Śāstry, chose to accompany Ekanāth on that pilgrimage to the root. They had so much to gain through the company of Śāṅtibrahma that they learnt all about the almost forgotten spiritual Quartet – Nivṛttināth, Jñānadev, Sopāndev and Muktāyi; all about the art of digesting the persecution of the society for no fault of theirs; and more importantly, about the art of transforming the base emotions to lofty feelings of forbearance, forgiveness, compassion, surrender and universal love.

□

2
The Precious Gifts

Dawn was yet to break. The world was preparing for a new day. Women cleaned the front of their homes; the menfolk waited to leave the homes for their morning ablutions; the cowherds were milking cows and children were getting ready for a new day of mischief, play and maybe, learning! A child, barely eight years old, had left his home with a shack of hay and leaves and away from the village on the other side of the hillock. After taking the dip in Indrāyaṇi river, he was slowly climbing the approach to the houses to collect *bhikṣā* - alms. In a sweet voice of a child, he sang:

> '*Living life of equanimity, by shattering the ego;*
> *This alone is the blessed way to attain the state of liberation.*'

The child opened his *jholi* in a gesture of asking for *bhikṣā* from a woman, who did not even take note of his existence. With a smile on his face, he proceeded to the next house, singing:

> '*Just as God does for his creation, nurture forgiveness in the heart;*
> *Meditate on that one principle alone.*
> *Name alone is the* maṅtra, *taking it without break one crosses over;*
> *Let no other thought enter one's being*!'[8]

---

8. समता वर्तावी, अहंता खंडावी; तेणेची पदवी मोक्ष मार्ग।

The woman was engrossed in drawing the Rangoli (floor decoration) when she noticed him and called her daughter to give him alms while murmuring to herself: "How can you refuse a beggar in the morning?" But warned the daughter not to touch the boy, lest they would lose their caste!

Accepting the alms gratefully, he headed further. Looking at him with disgust from a distance were three Brahmins commenting: "Here comes the sin of a *sanyāsi*; we should never cross his path for he is an ill omen."

The harsh comment could be heard by all, including the child who was unperturbed and continued walking after offering his *praṇāms* to the Brahmins. The child was Jñānadev, the second son of Viṭṭhalpant and Rukmiṇidevi. When he stood in front of another house, Visobāpant, the master of the house, arrogantly asked Jñānadev: "Why have you come to beg today?"

"My father is not well today," replied the child innocently.

"I hope and pray that your whole family falls sick and dies. This alone will absolve the hundred families of Āḷandi. Have I not told you not to come and beg at my home? Go away! Your shadow is desecrating my courtyard. Next time I see you, I will break your bones! Be off!"

Such an outburst was disturbing even for Jñānadev. Just as he was about to pass the house, he heard a shrill call, "Jñānadev!! Wait."

It was Namu, the daughter of Visobā, who was coming after him with alms. He stopped but said, without looking into her eyes, "I do not need any *bhikṣā* today."

"But why?"

"I do not feel like accepting it from this house."

"Am I an untouchable?" Namu asked innocently.

"No, you are not, but your respected father will be offended and angry if I do."

"*Bāḷ*[9] Jñānā!"

क्षमा धरी चित्ती, अखंड श्रीपती; एक तत्त्व चित्ती ध्यायी जे सू।
नाम हाची मन्त्रु नित्य नामे सार; दूसरा विचार घेवू नको।।

"Yes, *Āyī,*" Jñānadev responded spontaneously, looking in the direction of the call.

It was Sītābāī, Namu's mother. He said apologetically: "Forgive me; there was so much affection in your voice that I addressed you as *Āyī.*"[9]

"Why do you say so, Jñānā?" Sītābāī asked curiously.

"How can I, whose shadow desecrates even stones and soil, have the right to address you as *Āyī*?"

Drawing near him, Sītābāī smiled and caressing his cheek said: "You can call me *Āyī*. It appears you are angry. But why do you transfer that anger on to the whole family? Don't you think that it will hurt Namu if you do so?"

"Should one sacrifice one's happiness just not to hurt others?"

"Giving not much attention to one's own happiness for the sake of others is being human. *Bhūta-dayā, c*ompassion for all creatures, is Māṇus *dharma,* human law," Sītābāī said with much affection.

Jñānadev responded in joy: "Māṇus *dharma, bhūta-dayā*!! Yes, I shall accept the *bhikṣā* in all gratefulness!"

But it was not to be, for Visobā rushed out in extreme wrath at his wife, daughter and, of course, Jñānadev! He scolded both his wife and daughter and snatched the *jholi* to scatter whatever grain it contained and tore it. There were tears in the eyes of Sītābāī, Namu as well as Jñānadev, but Visoba's wrath did not permit him to feel the pain his action had caused.

In a pensive mood, Jñānadev started walking towards home. He had received the gift from his second *Āyī* – Sītābāī, about human law, though he had been stopped violently from receiving the *bhikṣā*. As he was about to cross the *ghāṭ,* Muktā, his four-year-old little sister, came rushing to him. His mother Rukmiṇidevi had come to fetch water. Looking at the crestfallen face of Jñānā, she asked: "Why are you sad, my child?" On noticing his torn *jholi* empty, she continued "Just

9. Marathi words for child and mother.

because you did not get *bhikṣā*? It does not matter if we do not eat today."

"No *Āyī*, you are tolerating much insult and loathing from the people. Are you not disturbed? Are you not sad? Is there no limit to your pain?"

Holding him to her bosom, she said: "My child, enduring misery with *samādhā*na, equipoise, and accepting whatever happens in life is *tapas*. It makes one strong and takes us towards God. Having *samādhāna* while enduring pain and misery is *tapas*!"

Jñānadev smiled at this gift from his mother! But his joy was shortlived. When Rukmiṇi approached the water front, she was not allowed to touch water. Someone broke her pot in anger. When Muktā rushed to her mother, a stone was pelted, hurting the child. Jñānadev tried to argue with the people but Rukmiṇi stopped him by telling him not to argue with elders.

They returned to their humble abode outside the village. Muktā rushed to her father and narrated what had happened. Viṭṭhalpant consoled her: "I realise that all of you have to suffer for no fault of yours. But perhaps, we are being tested for our capacity to endure! Kṛṣṇa says, in the *Bhagavad Gītā*: 'O son of Kuṅtī, the contacts between the senses and their objects, which give rise to the feelings of heat and cold, pleasure and pain, etc., are transitory and fleeting; therefore, Arjuna, endure them.' Arjuna, the wise man to whom pain and pleasure are alike and who is not tormented by these contacts, is eligible for immortality'."[10]

Jñānadev came and sat down near his father and started massaging his legs in devotion. He enquired, "*Bābā*, does it mean that all our so-called experiences are only temporary?"

Viṭṭhalpant responded in all affection: "Yes Jñānadev, everything is transent and fleeting!"

Jñānadev countered: "Then why do we get disturbed?"

---

10. मात्रास्पर्शास्तु कौन्तेय शीतोष्णसुखदु:खदा: । आगमापायिनोऽनित्यास्तांतितीक्षस्व भारत ।। श्रीमद्भगवद्गीता २.१४ ।।
यं हि न व्यथयन्त्येते पुरूषं पुरूषर्षभ। समदु:खसुखं धीरं सोऽमृतत्वाय कल्पते।। श्रीमद्गवद्गीता २.१५ ।।

"We take the world and ourselves to be eternal! It is only due to our ignorance."

As this dialogue continued, Rukmiṇi wondered whether the pangs of hunger were also temporal; the continuous persecution by the society was also fleeting? ...

Rukmiṇi started remembering her father Siddheśwarpant, who had been impressed by total trust in scriptures, the scholarly erudition and most of all, the basic sincerity towards the purpose of life in Viṭṭhalpant. They had married but Viṭṭhalpant could not put his heart into *gṛhastāśrama*. His soul pined for realisation of the truths he had mastered intellectually. And so, after taking the permission of his wife and her parents, Viṭṭhalpant set forth on a pilgrimage to Vārāṇasī, the city of lights. His wife had willingly and happily agreed for she knew that he would succeed in his mission and moreover, she could never be a hindrance in his life. But she had also urged him to return as soon as possible.

At Kāśī, he met Swāmi Rāmānanda, who accepted him as his disciple. After assessing the depth of the intensity of his yearning for Truth, Rāmānanda enquired about his marital status. In his over-enthusiasm to embrace *sanyāsa*, Viṭṭhalpant told his master that he was a *brahmacāri*, hiding the fact that he was married, and thus was initiated into *sanyāsa.* Viṭṭhalpant did gain what he wanted most – wisdom and experience but apparently, the small untruth would cost him and his family very dearly. Moreover, Providence had planned otherwise.

During his pilgrimage, Swāmi Rāmānanda stayed in Āḷandi for a few days. When Rukmiṇi offered her respects to him, he spontaneously blessed her with children. She smiled and explained that she had not smiled at the blessings but at her misfortune, for she was leading the life of a widow in spite of having a husband who had gone to Kāśī; some people had told her that he had embraced *sanyāsa*. Rāmānanda kept silent for a while but observed within that this lady was to be a mother of four illustrious children. The saint promised her that he would search out her husband and send him back to Āḷandi.

When he asked her about her husband's nature and appearance, her friend had told that he was of fair complexion; she told him about his lean structure and that his name was Viṭṭhalpant. She described him to be a shy seeker who seldom spoke. The saint wondered whether it could be one of his disciples, who went by the name of Caitanya, to be the husband of this lady. Rāmānanda assured her that his blessings would never remain unfulfilled and that she would have worthy children.

Soon after his return, Rāmānanda called his disciple by his real name Viṭṭhala who, in turn, was struck by the blow of Providence, making him feel embarrassed and repentant. He faced the righteous anger of his *guru*, who told him that a lie uttered with all noble intentions was still a lie and could never take anyone towards Truth. It was really cruel to leave a young wife to her fate and seek salvation, which is always a result of pure and righteous actions. Viṭṭhalpant, invaded by many strong emotions – remorse, guilt and sorrow – remained silent, with his head lowered. Looking at his silent disciple, the saint's anger cooled and he commanded him to return to *ghṛhastāśrama*. So Caitanya had to abandon his *aśrama* and return to Āḷandi and his devoted wife Rukmiṇi.

To Rukmiṇi's joy, her husband had returned! Amidst celebrations on the return of Rukmiṇi's husband, a *dharma sabhā* with a group of scholarly Brahmins, who were the custodians of tradition, took the decision that Viṭṭhalpant should be ostracised from the community as he had abandoned *sanyāsāśrama* to return to *gṛhastāśrama*.

Both husband and wife had to accept this cruel decision. In the hut, away from the village, they started their life. Viṭṭhalpant and Rukmiṇi continued leading an austere life of penance amidst all difficulties. Meanwhile, the society did not spare any effort to make their life miserable!

When their first baby boy Nivṛtti was born, they felt their

life was blessed indeed! The couple was further blessed with two more boys – Jñānadev, Sopān and a girl, Muktā.

These children turned out to be extremely patient, calm and least demanding. It was like a man getting the light of distant stars on a moonless night!

Due to the persecution and living on half or fully-empty stomachs, forced Viṭṭhalpant to think of some means to get permission from the elders. Jñānadev suggested that perhaps, if the whole family went round the nearby mountain Brahma Giri, their troubles would cease. Instead, they lost their first child Nivṛtti to a tiger who decamped with him. This loss constantly pricked Rukmiṇi like a thorn in the foot. Just then she heard a shrill voice: "*Alak Nirańjan*![11]"

It brought her back to the present reality! She rushed out to meet the saint and to her joy, it turned out to be Nivṛtti, his eyes bright and illumined with wisdom. He had transformed himself into Nivṛttināth. There was an ethereal spiritual glow on his face and being. Spontaneously, she cried out: "Hari! Look who is here!"

The whole family was reunited once again. Looking at her husband, Rukmiṇi said smilingly: "You are right! Our so-called misery is temporal indeed!"

In her eagerness she did not consider the other face of misery – happiness, which too is evanescent! Though there was apparent joy at family reunion, there was turmoil in the mind of Viṭṭhalpant. No doubt he had the experiential understanding of the *Śāstras*, but the worm of guilt was eating his vitals. Repentance constantly weighed upon his being. He knew that he was let down by his own understanding as it had made him lie to his *guru*. He was not convinced of the excuse of his over-enthusiasm to embrace *sanyāsa*. He felt helpless and distressed and felt at loss to even think of the next course of action. His brow showed the determination and decision he then took – not to prolong the persecution of his offspring.

---

11. This is how the wandering monks of Nāth tradition wish, which means Truth is unattached and is ever pure.

Looking at Rukmiṇi, he declared: "Let me approach the *dharma sabhā* and seek their permission for the *yajñopavit saṁskāra* of our sons."

"Wait." Rukmiṇi followed her husband. This time, she did not want him to go out alone.

Moonlight seeped through the leaves, creating magical patterns of light and shade on the ground. The sound of the hoots of owls was caught by the ears. A cool mild breeze caressed the skin with its nip creating goosepimples. Fragrance of jasmine greeted the nostrils. River Indrāyaṇi flowed incessantly nearby. On the verandah of the small hut, sat Nivṛttināth, wondering at the whereabouts of his parents. An hour before he had woken up with a shiver due to a cold breeze. He noticed that the door was ajar. When he walked towards it, he found his father's bed empty; perhaps, thought Nivṛtti, he had gone out. Returning to his bed, he adjusted the cover on Sopān. Jñānā was as usual in deep sleep, nothing could affect him – neither cold nor heat! But when his eyes fell on Muktā, he noticed that the place next to her was empty. He asked "Where is *Āyī*?" He was indeed worried. But then, he reasoned that perhaps both of them had gone out.

Without wanting to go back to sleep, he decided to come out and wait for them in the verandah.

As a habit, Jñānā never changed his position after falling asleep! When the first cock crowed, he woke up, to find his right hand resting on the bookstand that held the *Bhagavad Gītā*. The scripture was open on the page that contained the verses his respected father had chanted a few days back. Offering his morning prayers and also to the *Gītā*, he got up. When he looked around, he found the beds of his parents and the elder brother empty. Coming out of the hut, he found his brother sitting. He asked: "Why are you sitting outside *Dādā*?"

Looking at his younger brother affectionately, he said: "I am waiting for *Āyī-Bābā*. I wonder where they have gone." There was concern in his tone.

Suddenly, Jñānā remembered the events that had passed

in the past two days. He knew that the parents had approached the *dharma sabhā* for permission to perform the *yajñopavit saṁskāra*. On their return, they had spoken in whispers.

He had overheard one word *'dehāṅta'* to be the only condition put by the elders. The wonderful love and concern that both of them had showered upon the siblings – *Āyī* had fed each one of them with her hands and her instructions to Sopān and Muktā to never trouble Nivrttidādā and Jñānadādā. He had wondered, ''why?' as all had been extremely happy after this grand family reunion. Jñānā realised that all these were signs of his parents obeying the dictates of the *dharma sabhā*. It was then that *'dehāṅta'* struck him like lightning.

The child in Jñānā was evoked and he cried and cried on the loss of his dear parents. Concerned, Nivṛtti came near with all care to console and offered his shoulder to Jñānā and allowed him to cry. After all, Jñānā was only eight-years old, but Nivṛtti recalled his experience of the agelessness of *ātman* (the soul)! Jñānā told him his thoughts and his conclusion that the parents had made an extreme sacrifice for the sake of the future of their children. Once again, Jñānā broke down, unable to control his emotions. Listening to his younger sibling in all sympathy, Nivṛttināth embraced his dear brother silently, without uttering a word. In that embrace, Nivṛttināth transferred the realisation he had received from his respected *guru*, Gahininàth that the *ātman* is deathless and ever pure. Jñānā was consoled and was at peace. Both of them were ready to take upon themselves the task of bringing up their siblings, Sopān and Muktā.

Meanwhile, the horizon blushed and the birds had started saying their morning prayers. Jñāna got up to take on the responsibility. He said, "*Dādā*, I will look after the kitchen, but the task of teaching all of us, what you have learnt and experienced, will be yours."

Nivṛtti said with a smile, "Let us both nurture Sopān and Muktā. God has given us this task. Let us perform it with sincerity and devotion. Through His grace, I shall endeavour to share my experiences with you."

One more and very important phase of their life – learning and expanding the horizons of their understanding and experience – had begun. It would be tough, what with the whole village being against them, but as always, in spite of the fact that almost all the doors were closed, one or two windows were open to them in the form of Sītābāī and a handful of her friends. Namu would be the errand girl, who would deliver this family from starvation.

News spread like wild fire about the ending of life by Viṭṭhalpant and Rukmiṇidevi, the ostracised couple. Many opinions were voiced: some claimed that they should have taken their sins, their children with them; others were neutral for they did not want to be on the side of either justice or sin; some others were guarded but sympathetic; while others were openly critical of the heartless justice meted out by the so-called custodians of *dharma* for orphaning the children.

Visoba was one of the main persons who argued that if such actions were to go unpunished, the whole society would crumble. Unfortunately, the so-called *dharma sabhā* had forgotten that *dharma* without patience, sympathy, compassion and forgiveness cannot be called as real *dharma.* How were they to know and understand when they were obsessed only by the words in the scriptures, and not their spirit; and that the rules and dictums are for the freedom to grow, for the subjects to transcend the boundaries of division?

Viṭṭhalpant was overpowered by remorse, guilt and repentance, but he surrendered to the then society with the hope that his children would be spared. Rukmiṇidevi was deluged by worry and concern for her offspring while facing hatred and anger from the society, but accepted them and surrendered to the Lord and her husband to accompany him in death. Jñānadev faced hatred, disgust and neglect and most of all, sadness, but by accepting them as *tapas*, he tried to understand Māṇus *dharma.* Nivṛttināth, on the other hand, was detached and free due to his receptiveness for receiving the spirituality and benediction from his *guru*, Gahinināth. He could see through the drama Providence played to make them instrumental for a greater cause than mere survival. Thus it was that a family, which had to confront the vicissitudes, was able to transform the negative emotions pelted upon them by the society into totally sublime emotions of surrender, acceptance, patience, forgiveness, compassion and love.

□

3
Survival and Beyond

Rays of the late morning sun peeped through the gaps in the thatched roof, lighting the hearth lit by Jñānadev. It had taken him quite some time to gather the wood, to arrange the twigs first and then the smaller pieces of wood to light the fire. He remembered how Āyī used to patiently do this with so much of devotion, while chanting the name of 'Hari'. Even on just listening to that hum of his dear mother in his mind, he felt rested in body and mind. A *poḷi* (*roti*) and the curry of available greens in the vicinity were more than sufficient to quieten their gastric fire! It was not just food but much of concern and love that had been its principal ingredients. He decided that he too must follow her method and try to nourish his siblings. A spontaneous *abhaṅg* sprang out of his mouth:

> *'One, who stands in front of God's door for a while, gets the four emancipations.*
> *Chant Hari through the mouth repeatedly, the acquired* puṇya *has no limit.*
> *Remaining in the* saṁsāra *let the tongue be active with God's name.*
> *Then all the time the* Vedas *and scriptures will be standing by your side.*
> *Chant Hari through the mouth repeatedly,*

the acquired puṇya *has no limit.'*[12]

Nivṛttināth, sitting in the corner in front of the image of Lord Viṭṭhala, was attracted by the sweet voice of Jñānadev. He listened to it carefully. There was so much of ease and grace in it that Nivṛttināth felt blessed to have such a younger brother. Jñānadev went out to look out for Sopān and Muktāyi, who were playing outside. Muktā was watering the sapling of jasmine she had planted. On seeing Jñānadev, she said: "Jñāndādā, look the plant has two new leaves!!" There was excitement and appreciation in her voice.

"Yes Muktāyi, with everyday care, it will one day give you blossoms."

Muktā responded by looking at the plant lovingly: "Jñāndādā, this whole place will be filled with the fragrance!"

Sopān, not far away from them, asked: "*Dādā*, is it the same with the vision of God?"

Jñānadev said in all appreciation: "It is so, Sopān. You have to plant the seed of God's name in your mind, nourish it with the water of devotion and remove the weeds of unwanted thoughts. Nivṛtti *Dādā* will teach us how to do it. Are you not hungry? Come let me give you something." He lovingly brought them inside to give them a plantain each. Nivṛtti observed how Jñānadev was playing the role of Āyī so well that his younger siblings were getting ready for their life and its challenges ahead.

It appears quite unnatural for children of age four, six and eight years to discuss God. But they were no ordinary children; they all were prodigies. Viṭṭhalpant, their father, was alleged by the so-called custodians of *dharma*, of digressing from the *aśrama dharma*, that is, of returning from *sanyāsāśrama* to *gṛhastāśrama*, forgetting that Lord Śiva had married Umā after vanquishing the God of love with his third eye (the eye

---

12. देवाचिये द्वारी उभा क्षणभरी। तेणे मुक्तिचारी साधीयेल्या।। हरी मुखे म्हणा हरी मुखे म्हणा। पुण्याची गणना कोण करी।।
असोनि संसारी जिव्हे वेगु करी। वेदशास्त्र उभारी बाह्या सदा।। हरी मुखे म्हणा हरी मुखे म्हणा। पुण्याची गणना कोण करी।।

of wisdom).[13] The combination of his maturity, gained from the experiential insights into the scriptures when he was with Swāmi Rāmānanda while Rukmiṇidevi's devotion and patience had brought these children into this world. In spite of the struggle for survival, Viṭṭhalpant had spent most of his time chanting, explaining and discussing the scriptures and also his experiences with his family, infusing a taste for the life Divine. Moreover, these children were totally unscathed by worldliness, thanks to the society that had ostracised them!

Jñānadev, who had taken on the responsibility of a mother of the family, took his *jholi* and started walking towards the town, leaving Sopān and Muktāyi behind. As he set out, on his lips were the verses from *Śrīmad Bhagavad Gītā*:

> *'He who is not a source of annoyance to the world,*
> *who never feels offended with the world,*
> *who is free from delight and anger, perturbation and fear,*
> *is dear to me.'*[14]

He climbed the small hillock to reach the top. He felt at ease as his eyes fell on the tower of the temple of Siddheśwara, the Lord of Siddhas, in whom he had total trust. Going around the town and standing in front of a few houses, he did not get any alms. Still, he did not feel discouraged. Jñānadev continued chanting the verses from the *Gītā*:

> *'He who craves for nothing, is both internally and externally*
> *pure, is efficient, impartial,*
> *and is indifferent to all distractions,*

---

13. What yogic sport of Śiva is this? He sustains the world with two eyes, and destroys it with one eye of fire on forehead,
Why does he allow Umā to occupy half of his body in harmony after vanquishing Madana, the God of love?
No fear from Gowri when Cupid had been vanquished. Pleased became Śiva on Gowri as she was helpful,
No fear likewise from family when you are above lust; it is your companion on the path – Mankuthimma; 614; *Thus Sang Mankuthimma*, by A Narasimha Bhat, Asheervad Publications, Kasargod, 1993, pp-77-78.

14. यस्मन्नोद्विजते लोको लोकान्नोद्विजते च यः। हर्षामर्षभयोद्वेगैर्मुक्तो यः स च मे प्रिये।। १२.१५।।

who renounces the feeling of doer-ship in all undertakings
– that devotee is dear to me.
He neither rejoices nor hates, nor grieves nor desires,
who renounces both good and evil,
is full of devotion to me,
is dear to me.'[15]

Just then a stone hit him on the left shoulder and some slushy mud on his clothes. When he looked back in the direction from where they were thrown, he saw a few children – some of his own age and others older. The calm and composed mood was shattered and he was hurt both physically and mentally. He asked, pain writ over his being, "What have we done to deserve this?" They laughed in glee and kept staring at him.

The persecuting children felt they had succeeded in their mission of seeing the son of *sanyāsi* become miserable, but the fact was something else. Jñānadev was disappointed and pained because the verses he was chanting had not yet become part of his being but were only part of his memory! Jñānadev rushed into the hut and closed the door.

Muktā had seen her Jñāna *Dādā* returning empty-handed and disturbed. She came rushing behind but found the door closed. In spite of her calling and entreating him, he did not open the door. She started singing: '*Leave behind worry and anger,*

open the door O Jñāneśwara.
Yogis are of pure mind and tolerate the wrong doings of the world,
If the universe emits the flames of attachment,
Saints transform into water of bliss to quench them.
Someone's words or action hurled to hurt
Take them to be advice for self-growth.
Universe is only a puppet,
while Brahma is the controlling thread.
Open the door O Jñāneśwara."[16]

---

15. अनपेक्ष शुचिर्दक्ष उदासीनो गतव्यथः। सर्वारम्भपरित्यागी यो मद्भक्तः स मे प्रियः।। १२.१६।।
यो न हृष्यति न द्वेष्टि न शोचति न कांक्षति। शुभाशुभपरित्यागी भक्तिमान्यः स मे प्रियः।। १२.१७।।

16. चिंता क्रोध मागे सारा। ताटी उगडा ज्ञानेश्वरा।। धृ।।

By the time Muktā had finished singing, Jñānadev came out, recovered and with a smile on his face. The little sister had helped him wade through his mood. When she rushed to him, he held her close and said: "Muktāyi, you have opened my eyes! Are you hungry?"

She replied innocently: "Yes, but I can bear it. Moreover, we have water to drink!"

He hugged her, but his eyes were moist. Just then, a shrill voice could be heard; it was Namu, "Come! *Āyi* has sent some food for all of you!"

"Hari, Hari..." Nivṛtti whispered.

So far, he had been witnessing the whole play. Now he was more than convinced that God was with them! Guru Gahininăth had told him that all the four of them – three brothers and a sister – had very important roles to play. To his joy, he discovered that all his siblings were more than eligible for the wisdom he was to share with them. Nivṛtti would start playing his role in the spiritual resurgence. He had started preparing for this task soon after his return and he had practiced continually amidst all trials hit upon the family. Looking affectionately at his brothers, sister and a new-found sister who had brought them food, he smiled and walked towards them. It was the first day of the bright fortnight of the month. This night would be ideal for him to start his mission, he thought.

It was the practice of Nivṛttināth to spend every morning and evening in meditation on the bank of Iṅdrāyaṇi. Today, he had received the directive from his *guru* that he was ready to start sharing his wisdom with Jñānadev. It was the sixth *prahar.*[17] The moon had risen and its first crescent was visible. Sopān and Muktāyi were fast asleep inside the hut and Jñānadev was waiting for his dear brother's arrival. Involved as he was in the

---

योगी पावनी मनाचा। साही अपराध जनाचा।। १।।
विश्व रागे झाले वन्ही। सन्ते सुखे व्हावे पाणी।। २।।
शब्द शस्त्रे झाले क्लेश। संती मानावा उपदेश।। ३।।
विश्वपट ब्रह्मदोरा। ताटी उगडा ज्ञानेश्वरा।। ४।।

17. A day is divided into eight *prahars* of three hours each.

appreciation of Nature, he did not notice Nivṛttināth joining him, who asked: "Jñānā, why are you standing?"

Jñānā responded:

'*Dādā, the first crescent of the moon,*
Looking at it with full attention,
This cascade of nectar, how can one describe it?
I was absorbing the moonbeams through my body,
I was drinking this beauty with these eyes!'[18]

"Jñānadev, brother, you are a born poet! You are indeed blessed by Goddess Śāradā." In that moment, they both experienced a strange intimacy – a brotherhood not limited to blood, but was all encompassing, as if the entire Existence was making them understand that they were inseparable from it!

They sat facing each other under a tree. A pleasant mild breeze started blowing, carrying with it the fragrance of *tulsi* (basil leaf). They heard a hoot of an owl, a few crickets constantly chattering and a cuckoo continually calling for its mate. Amidst such sylvan milieu, Nivṛttināth started communicating: "Jñānā, *Nāthasaṁpradāya* – the tradition of Nāth *yogis* has chosen me as a conduit to pass on the wisdom discovered and realised by them. Our great grandfather was initiated by Guru Gorakṣanāth. It was his good deeds and grace that I was called by my *guru*, Gahininināth. What I was asked to share with you is quite simple, but to understand and digest it requires preparation."

He paused, as if waiting for Jñānadev to ask: "*Dādā*, if it is simple, why should we complicate it in the name of preparation?"

Nivṛttināth smiled and responded: "Too much of involvement with this world complicates our mind. Let me clarify it. We, most of us, are taking this world too seriously due to which we nurture attachment, which in turn begets infatuation, irritation, anger and other emotions. This

18. पाडियाची चन्द्रलेखा, ती पूर्णमानस वेखा। अमृताचि या अभिशेखा, या केउु ते म्हणावे ?
जरा चान्दणा अंगावर घेतो, हे सौन्दर्य हे डोळ्यानी पीडून घेतो।।

indulgence – of the body and senses, and involvement of the mind, diverts a lot of our energy.[19] Consequently, our mind gets confused and complicated! We have to only make the body relaxed, breath steady and mind calm. When we succeed in doing so, we become simple and can easily understand the Truth, which is simple!

"The first instrument we perceive is our physical body. It has to be fit because, if it is not, all our attention will be only on the body. When can we say that we are healthy?"

Jñānadev responded: "We are healthy when we are not conscious of it because we are conscious of our stomach only if it is aching!"

Nivṛttināth laughed happily. "Our search begins with the body when we become free from any discomfort or disease. Jñānā, I will now share with you what I learnt from my *guru,* Gahininàth – how to make our body stable and comfortable.[20] Remember, we should never use any force. Keeping your back, neck and head straight, sit in a posture which is natural for you."

"Gurudev, is this, all right?" Jñānadev, who was already seated in a cross-legged posture, asked, by just straightening his back, neck and head. Nivṛttināth noted that he had been addressed as Gurudev, and marvelled at the alertness of his younger brother.

"Yes, but you should be able to sit for long periods of time. You will be able to, when you start relaxing your effort. Initially, when you begin the practice, after some time the body starts complaining, through either restlessness or pain. By not cooperating with the restlessness, the mind becomes steady. And by enduring the pain, you develop *titīkṣā* (forbearance)."

Jñānadev asked: "How does one achieve that?"

Nivṛttināth continued: "You realise it by relaxing the

19. ध्यायतो विषयान्पुंसः सङ्गस्तेषूपजायते। सङ्गात्संजायते कामः कामात्क्रोधोऽभिजायते।। २.६२।।
क्रोधाद्भवति संमोहः संमोहात्स्मृतिविभ्रमः। स्मृतिभ्रंशाद् बुद्धिनाशो बुद्धिनाशात्प्रणश्यति।। २.६३।।
श्रीमगवद्गीता।।

20. स्थिरसुखमासनम्।। योगदर्शनम् २.४६।।

effort and by fixing the mind on *anaṅta*, expansiveness.[21] When the posture becomes effortless, you transcend the body awareness. Our great grand *guru*, Gorakṣanāth, discovered many postures by observing animals, birds as well as reptiles. These help us to relax and accept any and all situations in life! Now let us go deeper into the discussion. You said that we are conscious; how are we conscious?"

Noticing that Jñānadev had not understood the question, he continued: "What I mean is we are sitting here, but we are conscious of the breeze touching our skin, the sounds of crickets and birds, of the crescent moon which you described so poetically. And of course, we are also listening and sharing knowledge."

Jñānadev's eyes lit up when he said: "It is because of our *jñānendriyas*, the five senses that are gathering the five external sense objects that we perceive. Whereas, *karmendriyas*, the five senses of action, react to the external objects, made of *pancabhūtas*, the five elements.[22] We are not conscious of all the objects but of only those objects, which we pay attention to."

Both the brothers were silent for some time; then Nivṛttināth continued: "Jñānā, the act of being conscious or of reacting utilises the same energy which has been called as *prāṇa* or *śakti*, the vital energy. If one becomes aware of this, then he can control the senses as well as the reactions. You may ask why the control of *jñānendriyas* and reactions of *karmendriyas* are necessary? The mind is affected by the senses and their respective objects; when the senses are controlled, the reactions also reduce. Breath is the bridge that connects the body, of which we are aware and which is actually a manifestation of the *prāṇa*. Once again, the process is the

---

21. प्रयत्नशैथिल्य अनन्तसमापत्तिभ्याम्।। योगदर्शनम् २.४७।।

22. Nose, tongue, eyes, ears, and skin are the *jñānendriyas*, and hands, legs, tongue, organs of excretion and generation are the *karmendriyas* which react to *jñānendriyas*. The objects are formed by the *pancabhūtas* – the *earth* (smell), water (taste), fire (form), air (touch) and space (sound) and their combination.

same: become aware of the incoming breath and outgoing breath. For some time, you just be attentive to the breath, without changing anything."

Jñānadev could easily grasp and dive deep into the practice. And so, the transfer of ancient wisdom in which our *ṛṣis* had spent a lifetime in discovering the methods of realisation had begun.

Both were not conscious of the passage of time, but they were brought back to the normal reality with the first crow of a cock in the village! Jñānadev was extremely happy and exclaimed: "Gurudev, I feel refreshed and energetic and we did not sleep throughout the night!"

"Yes Jñānā, we were in a much more restful state than the normal sleep! We shall learn even deeper aspects of *sādhanā*."

Jñānadev, who fell prostrate, was showered with affectionate blessings by his elder brother, who was also his *guru*! Jñānadev got ready for the daily chores and also for the role of being a mother to his younger siblings.

At Āḷandi, a few families started feeling an itch of conscience. They began to ask themselves and also others, whether the act of persecution of innocent children of Viṭṭhalpant and Rukmiṇidevi was right and justified! Some even went to the extent of asking the members of the *dharma sabhā* that if even the persons who had converted to other religions could return to the original fold through *śuddhikriyā* (purification), why should the offspring of a *sannyāsi* couple, who had done enough *prāyascita* (penance of repentance) by ending their lives be left to suffer for no fault of theirs? But the custodians of the *dharma sabhā* did not heed; instead, they blamed the sympathisers of becoming part of *adharma*! However, the women, the mothers, took the cue and started sending enough food to the children, and who in turn got more time, in channelising their valuable energy towards the search.

In spite of the fact that the spiritual Quartet – Nivṛttināth, Jñānadev, Sopān and Muktāyi, had been orphaned by Providence, their total lack of complaint, innocence, guilelessness and purity had earned them multiple mothers and sisters. Nivṛttināth was more than convinced that the hearts of women had that all-encompassing love, which could accept any child without any prejudice of its origin, caste or creed. Thus, it came to be that the better half of the society that continued to persecute them became favourable confidants to the Quartet. Now it was for these prodigies to gain inner strength and vitality to fulfil the mission of their life – reach out to the so-called common lot to discover the jewel that resides within every heart.

□

4
The Search

The Indrāyaṇi river was in spate after the monsoon. Jñānadev sat under a tree after having a quick dip. When he looked at the flow, he felt as if she was trying to give him a message. In that roar of flowing water, he heard her say, 'Your heart too will be flooded – not by reactions, but by response of love and compassion. You have a great task ahead of performing *tapas*.'

He offered his salutations by bowing his head. His *guru* had started to work on him and the success depended solely on his receptivity and sincerity. He said loudly, addressing her, "Grant us your blessings *Māyi* so that we can become eligible for the benediction. *Jai Jai Rāmakṛṣṇa Hari*!!" When he uttered these words, the flow rose higher to hit a boulder nearby, splashing a little water on to his head. Jñānadev was convinced that she too was their comrade at arms!

When he reached the hut, he saw Muktāyi sweeping the floor. Sopān came out with a small earthen pot and started walking towards the river; a concerned Jñānadev said: "Wait Sopān, I too shall come with you."

Sopān stopped and said, looking into his elder brother's eyes: "Are you worried about my safety? Indrāyaṇi *Māyi* will never harm me!"

Amused, Jñānadev asked with a smile: "Why do you say that?"

"*Dādā*, she can never harm us because *Āyi* and *Bābā* are with her!"

Touched by the quality of the total trust in his younger brother, Jñānadev went near him and hugged him. His eyes moist and voice choked, responded: "I know you are very brave! But the water you will bring in that small pot will not be sufficient for us. I will bring two bigger pots."

As he entered the hut, he saw the benign face of his *guru* radiating spiritual energy. Nivṛttināth was in deep meditation. He prostrated and when about to get up, he heard his sister tiptoeing towards him without disturbing the meditation of her Nivṛtti *Dādā*. She too picked up a small pot and came out with her Jñāndādā. She whispered: "I too shall come to the river to fetch some water."

"Come, let us go!"

Jñānadev remembered an episode from *Śrīmad Bhāgavatam,* which his *Bābā* had narrated. Avadhūta Dutta, the son of sage Atri had twenty-four *gurus*. Most of them were animals, birds or insects and only a few human beings out of whom one was a little girl, a little older than Muktā. As they started walking towards the river, he asked: "Do you want to hear a story?"

Both of them were happy and shouted happily. Jñāndādā had many stories to tell and they were always eager to listen!

"Yes, please tell us!"

"This was told by *Bābā*. When Avadhūta Dutta went for a *bhikṣā* in a village, he stood in front of the door and said, '*Bhavati bhikṣām dehi.*'

"A small girl like you came out and said 'My *Āyi* and *Bābā* are not at home, but please wait. I shall clean the rice and bring it to you.' As he waited, he heard the sound of the bangles. The sound went on reducing until everything was silent. Soon the girl came out and offered him uncooked rice. Dutta asked the girl, 'How is it that the initial sound of the bangles went on reducing, until there was silence?' The girl said bashfully,

'When I started husking, so much noise was made by my bangles that I felt it would disturb your meditative mood. So, I went on removing the bangles, one by one, until only one bangle remained on each wrist. Even these two touched each other sometimes, creating the noise. Finally, only one bangle remained on one wrist and after that, everything became quiet.' Datta bowed low and said that she had taught him a lesson.

"Dattātreya realised and acknowledged the great spiritual truth she had given him through her action. He exclaimed: 'Where many dwell, there is noise and quarrel, even when there are only two, there is a dialogue. That is why one must live in solitude, to enjoy being alone, like the bangle on a wrist of the maiden.'[23] Do you know why I remembered this story?" Jñānadev asked Muktāyi who replied innocently: "I do not know, *Dādā*!"

Smilingly Jñānadev continued: "You too did not disturb Nivṛttidādā in his meditation."

Muktā rejoined saying: "I felt so peaceful that I did not want to disturb it."

"You are so wise, Muktāyi. Yes, when someone is in the state of meditation, you come near that person and if you are sensitive, you too shall feel that peace in your own heart."

By this time, they had reached the river. They filled their pots according to their individual capacity and started returning to the hut. As they walked, Muktā noticed that her pot was making a lot of noise while Jñāndādā's pot made the least. She asked: "*Dādā*, why is it that my pot is making so much noise while yours is not producing noise?"

"Your pot contains less water while Sopān's pot has little more. And since I am older than both of you, my pots are full of water."

She observed in turn: "Isn't it the same with knowledge? I talk the most, while Sopān *Dādā* talks less. You speak only

---

23. वासे बहूनां कलहो भवेद्वार्ता द्वयोरपि। एक एव चरेत्तस्मात् कुमार्या इव कंकणः ।। श्रीमद्भागवतम् ११.९.१० ।।

when required, whereas Nivṛtti *Dādā* hardly speaks, even when I ask him something."

Jñānadev wondered at the power of observation of his little sister, who was wiser than even older men!

Providence was taking care of them as they received sufficient food that was brought affectionately by Namu. The loving mothers took turns to send it as no house felt any burden.

Nivṛttināth loved to share the age-old wisdom of yoga with Jñānadev, who absorbed it with sincerity and devotion. Once they both were unaware of the external world and were lost within the inner dimension. After a while, when they became aware of the material world, they noticed their younger siblings sitting near them, their eyes closed and breathing steadily! When the children were back to normal consciousness, Jñānadev asked: "I thought you were asleep; when did you come here?"

Muktāyi replied: "Nivṛtti *Dādā*, Jñāna *Dādā*, we have been coming for nearly six months! One day when we woke up in the middle of the night, we found you both missing. I called Sopān *Dādā* and told him that both of you were not in your beds. Worried and fearing that like *Āyi-Bābā* you too may have abandoned us, we came out and found you both, sitting under this tree, lost in meditation."

Sopān joined in: "*Dādā*, when we approached you, all our worries and concern vanished and we were immediately at peace. From that night on, we wait for both of you to lose yourselves within; then we approach you without disturbing your meditation. I sit near Nivṛtti *Dādā* and Muktāyi near Jñāna *Dādā*! Normally, we used to sit till we felt sleepy so that you would not be disturbed, but today we do not know how but we were so peaceful that we did not feel sleepy at all!"

Muktā said eagerly: "*Dādā*, I felt I had merged with the sky!"

Sopān too said, excitement not lacking in his voice: "Yes, I was able to see all the four of us sitting with our eyes closed, as if I was seeing us all from the sky! What was it that happened to us?"

Nivṛttināth and Jñānadev, who were pleasantly surprised, looked at each other with joy. Nivṛttināth gestured to Jñānadev to speak: "You are blessed indeed. No, all the four of us are blessed! It is due to the virtuous merits we received through our respected parents that we are what we are. It is a sure omen from God to tell us that for all the four of us, life is meant for something subtler, higher and nobler than ordinary life of survival. Gurudev, please tell them about the instructions of your *guru*, Gahininăth."

"My dear brothers and sister, Gurudev taught me the age-old wisdom he had received from his *guru*, Gorakṣanāth, with a command that it is meant for all the four of us and that together we will fulfil the purpose of our life. But I never expected that whatever we are sharing and learning will be so easily absorbed by you two! From now on, we shall perform our *sādhanā* together."

Muktāyi rejoined happily: "*Dādā*, we will call you Gurudev when we try to learn from you. We know that Jñāna *Dādā* addresses you that way. We shall learn whatever you teach us with utmost devotion."

With that, the spiritual Quartet merged as a unit to practice for the great music they were to bring to the world!

"*Dādā*, why does the society continue to persecute us?" Muktāyi asked Nivṛttināth, who looked at Jñānadev.

"For the welfare of the society certain rules are formed, telling us what actions we should perform and other actions that we should not. This keeps the society under discipline. Most persons follow the rules and when some do not, they have to face some disciplinary actions. But look at the brighter side. We have this golden opportunity to perform *sādhanā*, which has to be done only in solitude."

Jñānadev had succeeded in steering the attention in the

positive strain. There was silence for some time, then: "Why do we need to be in solitude, *Dādā*?" It was Sopān who asked this question.

Jñānadev smiled and responded: "When we are in the society, our mind gets involved with it through happenings and we take on the colour and mood of the society – excited, angry, worried or sad, whenever there is any cause for these reactions. Don't you remember the day when I had entered the hut and closed myself in? It was Muktāyi who made me aware of my foolishness!" He laughed happily at himself.

Nivṛttināth said in all appreciation: "Jñānā, when, instead of laughing at others' faults, we start laughing at our own, we enter the world of *adhyātma* (spirituality). May God bless you brother! From this moment on, we shall perform *tapas* as one single unit. We compliment and complete one another."

Looking into his siblings' eyes, he knew that he had to explain. He continued: "*Bābā* had been very thoughtful in naming each one of us. *Nivṛtti* means 'giving up lower activities for taking up higher pursuits. It results in *vairāgya* – disinterest in the material world that begets wisdom or *jñāna*. Remember Jñāna is not just knowledge which is only information, but is experiential that helps one to climb the steps – Sopān, to lead us to *mukti* (liberation). *Nivṛtti, Jñāna, Sopān* and *Muktā* are always together!"

They sat in silence for some time. Jñānadev got up to attend to the daily chores. Muktāyi joined him with full enthusiasm. Both of them collected wood for the hearth and swept the hut and its surroundings clean. Sopān joined them when they started to walk towards the river to fetch water. When they approached the water front, Jñānadev asked them to sit for a while. Looking at the turbulence of water, he started thinking. He had been initiated by his *guru* and he had also been practicing it in all sincerity and devotion. But he was yet to receive any sign of the progress he had made. He was aware that there was no place for impatience in spirituality, but still felt restless in his mind. Spontaneously, he started singing:

'Having come far off to distant land, my mind remembers you.
Don't want this separation, my soul is restlessly troubled.
O Mother, the day changed to night, and the night into day.
I have come a long way from home and remember you.
Not wanting this separation, my soul pines in pain,
Having abandoned me here, why don't you come?
O benign natured God please come riding on your eagle,
O Father Viṭṭhala, the companion of Rukmiṇidevi.'[24]

Both his younger siblings listened to him in rapt attention. Muktāyi's eyes were moist for she had caught the mood of the *abhaṅg*. Looking at her, Sopān, feeling that she was remembering their parents, caressed her head to console her.

She said, but her voice had joy in it: "Jñāna *Dādā*, by '*Bāpa Rakhumadevi varā Śrī Viṭṭhala*', do you mean *Āyi-Bābā*?"

Jñānadev was silent for a while and then said with all deliberation: "We came into this wonderful world through *Āyi-Bābā* and also received our *saṁskāras*, our basic nature, from them. But presently, all our needs are being looked after by Viṭṭhala, the husband of Rukmiṇidevi![25] We have to be grateful to all of them."

Muktāyi asked him in all seriousness: "*Dādā*, are you not complaining to God about the delay in giving you his *darśana*? Are we not supposed to not expect any fruits of our actions?"

Jñānadev and Sopān smiled at her observation: "What you say is true. Such expectations only give us more misery. However, there is another dimension when we make such

---

24. पडिलें दूरदेशीं मज आठवे मानसीं। नको हा वियोग कष्ट होताती जीवासि।। १।।
दिन तैसी रजनी झाली गे माये। पडिले दूर देसी मझ आठवे मानसी।। २।।
नको नको हा वियोग, कष्ट होताती जीवासी। अवस्था लावोनी गेला अजूनि का न ये।। ३।।
गरुड वाहना गुणगंभीरा एईगा दातारा। बाप रखुमादेवी वरा श्रीविट्ठला।। ४।।

25. Some of the *abhaṅgs* Jñānadev used this as his pen name, in some he used *Niyttidāsu,* in others, he used *Jñānadev.*

appeals to God. Tell me, when you are hungry, don't you ask me for some food? Why do you do that?"

Muktāyi responded spontaneously: "You have taken *Āyi's* place!"

"More than that, you consider me as very close to you. We ask for something only from those whom we consider very close to our heart. God is the closest to us, in fact, closer than we can ever imagine. But we are not aware of the closeness to him. So, by making such appeals to Him, we draw closer to Him; we become aware of that closeness! Come, we have to fill water in our pots and return to the hut."

Both Sopān and Muktāyi had received food for thought. God is closest to us, but we are unable to feel that closeness due to our own limitations. And we can feel that closeness through *sādhanā*. On their way back, Jñānadev started showing them the beauty of Nature: the sun seeping through the foliage of trees; the birds in flight; the blossoming flowers on bushes as well as ground; the restless flow of water of Iṅdrāyaṇi; the cranes feeding upon the small fish and insects; the steadiness of the intense look of the kingfisher before diving in for its prey in the river.

They also became aware of the softness of breeze brushing past their bodies; the call of a calf to its mother cow. The children had become aware of the beauty and were in all appreciation; they were not at all conscious of the weight of water pots upon their heads!

Jñānadev asked them as they reached the hut and had kept the pots on the floor: "Did you feel any strain while returning home?"

Muktāyi replied happily: "No *Dādā*, we were not even aware that we were carrying the water on our heads!"

Their elder brother remarked happily: "Do you know the reason why? It was because we were conscious of the beauty of this world which is created by God. Imagine how wonderful our life would be when we behold the Creator Himself!" He paused and then asked, "Muktāyi, are you watering the jasmine creeper?"

"Yes *Dādā*, every day without fail. But it has not yet started blossoming."

Jñānadev smiled and said: "My little sister, we will wait patiently for that day!"

Muktāyi asked innocently: "Can't we make an appeal to the creeper?"

"We cannot force the creeper, just as we cannot force God to give His *darśana,* but appeal we can! All we can do is to remain patiently alert and be ready for the benediction!"

The sky had turned violet in the west and the east was lit up with innumerable stars. A mild breeze was blowing, bringing with it the coolness as well as the hum of the river in flow. The Quartet sat under the *pīpal* tree for their *sādhanā*.

Nivṛttināth started talking: "An Upaniṣad declares in a maṅtra*:* He wished. 'Let me be many, let me be born.' He performed *tapas.* Having performed tapas, He created all this that exists. Having created all this, He entered into that very creation.'[26] God is without in all beings, *sthāvaram* (stationary) and *jangamam* (moving). Though God is surrounding us and also within us, we are unable to see Him. Not because He is not there, but because we are not with Him! Today, while returning from the river, you were able to see the beauty of Nature. It was there even before, but you started seeing it when you became conscious of it! He is, but we are unable to see or feel His presence."

There were no questions in the listeners' minds. After a pause, Nivṛttināth started speaking again, but it was as though his voice was one amongst the many natural sounds: "God IS, in everything we smell, taste, see, touch and hear. He IS, with us as our physical body, within us as the processes of circulation, respiration, digestion, etc.; our senses *jñānendriyas*

---

26. सोऽकामयत। बहु स्यां प्रजायेयेति। स तपोऽतप्यत। स तपस्तप्त्वा। इदं सर्वमसृजत्। यदिदं किंच। तत्सृष्ट्वा। तदेवानुप्राविशत्।। तैत्तिरीयोपनिषद् २.६.१।।

and *karmendriyas,* our emotional reactions like fear, anger and sadness, as well as our oneness, compassion, love and devotion, in anything that can be experienced."

There was a pause: "He IS our mind, intellect, memory and ego. Do you know why, in spite of His eternal presence, we are unable to feel or perceive Him? It is because we are not even aware of those very things which can be felt by our senses, mind, or conceived by our intellect. So initially we have to learn to be aware of day-to-day perceptions and actions."

Nivṛttināth had uttered the greatest Truth in an extremely simple language. He continued: "The *prajñā* can be developed through the process of yoga, which helps us to slowly increase our awareness from those very things we perceive and feel. Jñāna helped you to see the beauty in Nature when you were returning from Iṅdrāyaṇi *Māyi*."

He felt as though Muktāyi had something to ask, when he looked encouragingly, she said: "Gurudev, how did you know what we did today, when you did not even leave the hut?"

Nivṛttināth smiled and responded: "I do not have to leave the hut to know what is happening in the world. It is due to the grace of my *guru*, Gahinināth that I have this awareness. Moreover, as I told you, we are connected very intimately."

In that specific moment, they felt that they were a unit and what they heard was coming from a voice within. Instead of seeking any explanation for this experience, they all dived deeper within. From that moment onwards, together they started making effort in continuing to feel this intimacy.

Sopān asked a few days later, when they sat under the tree: "Gurudev, I am able to feel the oneness we had felt the other day, only when we are all together. But during other times when I am involved with the daily chores, it dissolves."

Jñānadev responded when Nivṛttināth looked at him: "Sopān, you may be giving too much attention to the body. While you are involved with the actions, the *prajñā* - awareness, goes into the background."

Feeling that Sopān had not understood, he continued: "Let me put it in a different way. When we are all together, we are under Gurudev's aura, and His power of *tapas* takes care of all of us! But when we are not with Him physically, somehow, we go back to our old ways due to age-old habit of indulging with the body, with the action or involving with our thoughts and emotions. We need to consciously remember that God is within as well as outside. He is always with us, and we are eternally in His embrace!"

There was a pause of silence. Then Muktāyi asked innocently: "But Jñān *Dādā*, I do not feel separate at all, from all of you!"

Nivṛttināth said with an indulgent smile: "Among us, Muktāyi, you were born free – free of fear, free of any inhibitions, free of any doubt! That was why *Āyi-Bābā* named you Muktā, which means liberated. You have to be only reminded about your real state and that is what I am doing."

Jñānadev looked at his sister lovingly and said: "Muktāyi, you are with us to inspire us to seek our own freedom and liberation."

"I do not know about that *Dādā*, but right now I am seeing Namutāyi climbing down the hillock with our food! Let us all be free from the thoughts about food!"

They all laughed at the comment. Jñānadev felt extremely grateful to his other sister Namu and, of course, mother Sītābāī and as usual, his eyes became moist. Nivṛttināth had been observing such responses from Jñānadev of becoming emotional so easily. Guru Gahininātha had told him that he had to help his sister and brothers to strengthen the qualities inherent to them. Jñānadev could feel so intensely that it manifested through the tears. The tears were not ordinary but pearls of expression of love, the love that could encompass the whole universe! Jñānadev would be the *heart* and *voice* of the Quartet. Sopān, on the other hand, though silent, was very observant. Extremely curious and alert, he could easily adopt many methods of mind control on his own. Nivṛttināth felt that he should share those methods with this younger brother. Sopān would be the *tapas* dimension of the Quartet and Muktāyi would be the *power* and the *force* of the Quartet.

□

5
Discovery and Benediction

Soft rays of the morning sun scattered through the foliage of the trees as rays of benediction. Before settling, the dust danced through those very rays as though Mother Earth was interacting with light! After spreading their wings and stretching their beaks, the birds had started their chatter as if sharing their dreams seen in the night. Though the sound they made was loud, it did not disturb the peace. Having sprinkled water on the ground after sweeping the ground, Jñānadev helped Muktāyi make *Rangoli* (floor decoration) in front of the hut. Just when it was being completed, a crow perching on the *pīpal* tree started cawing. Pointing it to his dear sister and looking affectionately at it, Jñānadev started singing, addressing it:

> *'O mother, the crow has brought an omen through his caw.*
> *Fly away, fly away O crow; I shall anoint your feet with gold,*
> *Tell me when is Panḍharīrāvu – Lord of Pandharpur coming.*
> *I shall feed you with curd-rice; tell me fast, the good news of His arrival!*
> *I will keep the cup of milk near your beak; tell me the truth my dear friend,*

When will Viṭṭhala grace us by his visit?'[27]

The crow heard the *abhaṅg*, then looked at them and flew away as though he had conveyed what he wanted to! Jñānadev smiled and kept looking in the direction it had flown. Muktāyi asked happily, and there was mischief in her tone: "*Dādā*, do you think the crow understood what you said to him?"

Caressing her back with affection Jñānadev replied: "Muktāyi, every being has a language of communication. It not only communicates with its own kind, but also with others. Perched on that tree, the crow tried to say something to us. I remembered the popular belief that if the crow perches near you and caws, a guest is coming. I responded with an *abhaṅg*. I feel he was listening, because he could have flown away any time, but he waited for me to finish!"

Jñānadev noticed his dear sister become serious when she said: "*Dādā*, I know that you have only one single thought and that of having the vision of God. Whatever you do, speak or think, you are always seeking Him and Him alone. *Tu dhanya āhe, Dādā* - you are indeed blessed. *He* will be at fault, if He does not give you the vision!"

Pressing his dear little sister to his heart, Jñānadev said with moist eyes: "No Muktāyi, the delay is never from His part, but always from the seeker's part. Don't you remember, Gurudev saying the other day that we are *always* enveloped by Him within and without? Moreover, *viraha* – pangs of separation help the mind never to forget the person we miss. Shall we go to Māyi Indrāyaṇi?"

It had been nearly one year since the Quartet had started their quest for the Divine. Nivṛttināth had almost completed sharing his wisdom with his brothers. He had succeeded in increasing the thirst in Jñānadev, and the habit of practice

---

27. पैल तो गे काऊ कोकताहे। शकुन गे माये सांगताहे।। १।।
उड उड रे काऊ तुझे सोन्यानें मढविन पाऊ। पाहुणे पंढरीरावो घरा कैं येती।। २।।
दहिंभाताची उंडी लाविन तुझे तोंडी। जीवापढिये त्याची गोडी सांग वेगी।। ३।।
दुधें भरुनी वाटी लावीन तुझे वोंठी। सत्य सान्गे गोठी विठो येयिल कायी।। ४।।

in Sopān. Muktā of course, had started remembering her freedom! One evening when they were sitting under the *pīpal* tree, he asked Jñānadev: "Jñānā, when you say you want to see God, what do you really mean by God?"

Jñānadev deliberated for a while before replying: "Gurudev, I have been seeing the images of Viṭṭhala and Rakhumāyi since childhood; for me therefore, they are the forms of God. I want to behold them; I want their vision." He was choked with emotion.

Nivṛttināth said empathetically: "Jñānā, you shall have the vision as you have imagined." Looking at Sopān he asked:"Sopān, I know that even while you eat, or are engaged in other daily chores, your mind is focused. What are you seeking, while you practice so ceaselessly and continually?"

Sopān just looked at his *guru* without replying. Nivṛttināth coaxed him with his eyes to speak.

"Gurudev, I want to increase my *prajñā*, to the extent that nothing escapes its sight!"

"You too shall achieve what you seek, my brother. Be patient and never be in a hurry! Come Muktāyi, let us take a walk by Iṅdrāyaṇi Māyi; let our brothers continue their quest."

When they were near the bank of the river, Muktā asked:

"Gurudev, when you blessed Jñān *Dādā* you added 'as you have imagined.' What did you mean?"

"You can call me, *Dādā*, as I have nothing to teach you and you have nothing to learn! Let us only be brother and sister! Now let us take that question of seeing God. Remember that, always we see only what we perceive. And our mind, our thought is behind our perception. Though Jñānā told you about my mentioning to you that we are enveloped by God within and without, he still thinks that God is separate, like Viṭṭhala and Rakhumāyi!"

He waited for Muktā to respond: "I am learning from you even now! You are helping me to remember! You are my *guru*!

But tell me... O I understand now. He IS within us, and all that is without. That means *we are He* and *He is us*!"

Suddenly, Muktāyi glowed as if lit from within. She laughed heartily on this great discovery. She fell at the feet of Nivṛttināth, who lifted her up. Strange as it may seem, but it was as though they had become one physically as well as spiritually! After some time, they started walking again.

Muktā said: "Gurudev, Sopān *Dādā* is also seeking the same thing when he said he is seeking *prajñā: God is prajñā* and *prajñā is God*!" The silence that followed was full and flowing like Iṅdrāyaṇi beside them.

A few days later, the dawn brought the new dawn for Jñānadev. He woke up very early and as was his wont, he first looked at the image of the Divine couple, Viṭṭhala-Rakhumāyi. The lamp lit their faces and as he continued to look at them, he saw them both smiling and raising their right hands in blessing. At first, he thought that perhaps it was only his imagination, but Viṭṭhala beckoned him to come closer. Rubbing his eyes he went near the pedestal. True, it was real! He was seeing them with his eyes open! Unable to restrain the tears of joy, nay ecstasy, Jñānadev fell prostrate, surrendering himself totally to them and remembered gratefully his parents, who had been their gate to this world.

He came out of the hut and to his pleasant surprise saw that the jasmine creeper had flowered its blossoms! As Muktāyi came out, she saw her Jñāna *Dādā* standing near her creeper. She too saw the blossoms of jasmine. When she came near him, Jñānadev burst out into an *abhaṅg*:

> *"A small sapling that was planted by the entrance;*
> *It has grown into a creeper, spreading into the infinite sky.*
> *Jasmine has blossomed, the jasmine has blossomed,*
> *The creeper is heavily laden with buds and blossoms.*
> *Knots of my mind have arranged themselves into a garland,*

It is offered to Father Viṭṭhala, the companion of Rakhumadevi."[28]

It was his first vision and Jñānadev was in ecstasy for the next week or so, as if he was lighter, as if the ground did not hold him! But soon the joy started waning, until he felt as if he was thrown on the ground! Emotional that Jñānadev was, he started missing the experience of the vision. He had never felt the misery he was experiencing as intensely at that particular point of time. He had tasted it, when their parents had left them, or when he was unable to feed Sopān and Mukta, or even when they were persecuted by the whole of Āḷandi. This was something totally different, as though his heart was being wrenched like a wet cloth. He had to share this with his *guru*.

In the evening, when Nivṛttināth returned from the river, Jñānadev rushed and fell at his feet. Nivṛttināth understood and asked Jñānadev to accompany him for a stroll on the hillock. As they climbed up and stood looking at the village of Āḷandi, a cool soft breeze blew as if consoling Jñānadev. They had not spoken, but Nivṛttināth could feel the burden in his dear brother's mind and the strain he was going through. He spoke as though his voice came through the breeze: "*Sādhu*! Only now your journey towards fulfilment has begun! My dear Jñānā, all these days you were only making preparations!"

"Gurudev, the pain is unbearable; I feel everything is petty and pointless, unless I see them again. Please help me to have that vision eternally!"

Nivṛttināth smiled and just pointed towards the setting sun, and then he asked: "Jñānā, what do you see?"

"Gurudev, a setting sun," replied Jñānadev, but he was clueless why this question was asked.

"You are seeing only the setting of the sun without seeing the beauty of this phenomenon! Usually, you never fail to see

---

28. इवलेसें रुप लावियले द्वारी। तयाचा वेलु गेला गगनावरी।। १।।
मोगरा फुलला, मोगरा फुलला। फुलें वेचितां अति भारु कळियासि आला।। २।।
मनाचिये गुंती गुंफियला शेला। बापरखुमादेविवरु विट्ठलीं अर्पिला।। ३।।

the beauty in everything around. Why don't you see it now?"

Jñānadev thought awhile and then responded: "My mind is involved with the memory of the experience! And it is stubbornly insisting on repeating. This activity is so intense that I am unable to behold the beauty of sunset."

"I will ask you another question: how did you have the vision of God?"

"Gurudev, I had it with these very eyes when they were wide open." Jñānadev wondered why such a question was asked, which had an obvious answer.

Again, Nivṛttināth asked: "For your eyes to see, your mind should be connected with them; then and then alone you are able to see. Your mind was constantly thinking and thinking intensely about Viṭṭhala-Rakhumāyi. So, when you had that experience, your mind and your eyes *together* saw the Divine couple. Now try to remember when or what was your mental state when you had the experience."

Now Jñānadev understood the background of this whole conversation! His eyes lit up when he burst out:"Yes, Gurudev, I had slept very peacefully that night and had a good night's rest. My mind was very peaceful, and without any previous thought of what I saw!"

Nivṛttināth was very happy that his dear brother was discovering the truth about experiences. He encouraged him by saying: "Good Jñānā, your mind was peaceful or in other words, it was without any activity as you rightly said earlier. Now I shall whisper a great spiritual truth: till you have the first experience, it is good to seek it with all your being, with focused and intense feelings. But after the first experience, you have to remember three very important facts: your mind has to be totally silent without any activity in which there is no expectation and the experience will never be repeated, just as this wonderful sunset is never repeated. Even tomorrow the sun will set, but it will be different! You shall have experiences but your first experience will never be repeated."

Jñānadev was consoled, his problem dissolved into thin air! He once again fell at the feet of his Guru Nivṛttināth, who said jovially: "Come, let us sit on this rock and enjoy the sunset while it lasts!"

The two brothers continued to sit, till they saw the last of the sun. As the western horizon turned red, the eastern horizon turned violet and then dark. They smelt the smoke from the hearths rising towards the zenith and saw the twinkling wonders appearing slowly.

Just then they heard: "Nivṛttidādā, Jñāna *Dādā,* it is *sandhyā,* let us pray!" It was Muktāyi calling out to her brothers.

It had become a strong habit for Sopān to spend most of the time under the tree. He could sit in *padmāsana,* the lotus posture for long durations without movement. Nivṛttināth was observing his younger brother quite keenly and was certain that he had achieved *āsanasiddhi,* mastery of the posture. He felt the time had come for him to speak to Sopān. Going near the tree that evening, he sat in front and slowly started speaking, without disturbing the mood of Sopān: "Sopān, I have noticed that you are able to spend long hours in the same posture without being conscious of your body.[29] When you close your eyes to meditate, what happens inside?"

As usual Sopān took time to respond to the question. He said: "Gurudev, initially my attention was on my breath. Then it got fixed on *prāṇa,* the principle, as you had kindly said, behind all activity. Presently, I am able to see that it is behind all activity within the body. It is giving me so much of joy that I do not want to get up from this seat!"

Nivṛttināth had the satisfaction to learn that this brother too had progressed and now it was time for him to take that next leap within. He spoke with a lot of affection: "Good

29. It is said that if one can sit for a minimum of three hours in the same posture without being conscious of the body, one has achieved *āsanasiddhi*. The purpose of *āsanā* is to transcend the body consciousness.

Sopān, though you have progressed, you should not stop, but proceed further. Now listen to me carefully."

A few noisy parrots were perched on the tree. Looking at Sopān, he knew that the noise of the parrots made no impression on Sopān. He continued: "Sopān, even this awareness of *prāṇa* is only a stage we pass through on our journey to the Divine. You have experienced that *prāṇa* is responsible for all the physical activities within the body. Let us start from there. Let us now become aware of another activity – the activity of the mind." As if the parrots too had received a cue from the master, they became still and quiet.

Soon as the attention of Sopān was drawn to the flow of thoughts, his awareness of *prāṇa* dwindled and went to the background. Since he was getting used to the awareness of *prāṇa*, he was a little disturbed. So he asked, full of concern in his voice: "But *Dādā*, is it not a fall? I was enjoying a silent mind, but now it is active again!"

Nivṛttināth responded with affection: "I will not allow you to fall Sopān, because I am holding you! Don't jump to any conclusion. I had told you never to be in a hurry! Observe for some more time, wait and watch."

Reassured, Sopān plunged within. After some time, he observed that the mind was nothing but a constant flow of thoughts and thus he experienced that mind too is an activity, just like *prāṇa*! He exclaimed: "*Dādā*, mind is also an activity like *prāṇa*. Forgive me, I addressed you as *Dādā*, Gurudev."

"I am your brother first, then only your preceptor. When you discover something, you want to share it with someone very close to you! You had a very rare experience and so you called me *Dādā*! But tell me, what does this experience mean to you now?"

Sopān relived what he had felt, and then responded: "Gurudev, it means that like any activity, the mind too can be stopped. It also means that since it resembles *prāṇa*, the mind too can be directed and controlled."

Nivṛttināth was satisfied that he had put this brother too in the right direction of progress. He added with pride in his heart and love in his voice: "Sopān, do not stop with this discovery, keep moving forward!"

A member of this Quartet was observing and aiding all the others in their progress – Muktāyi! She not only helped in the small simple household, but also in being with her elder brothers, Jñānadev and Sopān. For Nivṛttināth, she was a companion with whom he could discuss about the progress of his brothers. During these discussions, he would look within whether he had the experiential wisdom to guide his brothers in their spiritual progress. For Jñānadev, she was an inspiration for his spontaneous *abhaṅgs.* Just by looking at her guilelessness and her pure and calmly smiling countenance, his heart would take leaps within himself. And for Sopān, she was an understanding companion, sitting silently beside him, whenever she was free from work. Nivṛttināth's observation was correct – she was a *nityasiddha,* ever perfect and had only come to this world to aid them in their mission.

One morning after returning from the river, Jñānadev sat with Muktāyi, who was preparing a garland of jasmine flowers for her Viṭhoba and Rakhumāyi. His eyes fell on her tender fingers at work and then he had a sudden insight: what he was seeking was with him all along – God in this little sister of his. Then he saw that the collected blossoms; the fragrance emitted by the flowers; the tree behind her; the parrots perched on its branches; the gurgling sound made by Iṅdrāyaṇi; the river itself; the sun's rays pouring warmth; the warmth experienced by the skin; the person within who was seeing, listening, feeling and experiencing. He burst out into an *abhaṅg*:

'O Jñānā, you have become pure;
You have understood that you were meditating on self.
You are your own feelings; you are your own God;
And the doubt of otherness has dissolved.

Having crushed the mind, you have manifested in consciousness;
Your ways are unfathomable indeed O Lord.
All the lamps have started diminishing their light;
And all the wicks in the house have become non-existent.
The vṛttis, *modifications have turned to* nivṛtti, *renunciation within;*
Entire world has become the Vaikuṇṭha, the abode of Viṣṇu.
Nivṛtti, *you are ever in the Ultimate, in peace and compassion;*
It is due to your compassion that Jñānadev saw all this.'[30]

Just then Nivṛttināth came out of the hut; there was ecstasy, bliss on his countenance. His Jñānā had *seen*! Both Jñānadev and Muktāyi approached him and offered their grateful prostrations. Jñānadev said with his throat choked: "Gurudev, only now I have become eligible to fall at your feet. All along you had been trying to tell me but I did not comprehend. Perhaps I was impatient. And now I understand!"

Nivṛttināth blissfully lifted Jñānadev and said: "Jñānā, you are not an exception, we all forget how to feel Him through and through. You are right, in saying we are impatient."

Just then, they saw Sopān approaching them. They saw that his whole body glowed and his face had an ethereal smile. He came and fell at the feet of Nivṛttināth, who raised him and embraced him. Sopān said: "Gurudev, now I see that there is nothing other than consciousness. The wall that differentiates *sthāvaram*, the immovable and *jangamam*, the alive, has dissolved. Now there is only *prajñā*. I put so much effort that I wanted to achieve it as soon as possible! But your advice

---

30. अरे अरे ज्ञाना झालासी पावन। तुझे तुझ ध्यान कळो आले।। १।।
तुझा तूं चि देव तुझा तूं चि भाव। फिटला सन्देह अन्यतत्त्वाची।। २।।
मुरडूनियां मन उपजलासी चित्ते। कोठे तुझ रितें न दिसे राया।। ३।।
दीपक दीपक मावळल्या ज्योती। घरभरी वाती शून्य झाल्या।। ४।।
वृत्ती चि निवृत्ति अपणांसकट। अवघेंची वैकुंठ चतुर्भुज।। ५।।
निवृत्ति परमानुभव नेमा। शान्तिपूर्ण क्षमा ज्ञानदेवो।। ६।।

never to be in a hurry and practise *śama*, to be as patient as possible, changed my attitude. The first thing I learnt was that mind and *prāṇa* are just two aspects of the same principle. When I was in *prāṇa,* I was not conscious of the mental *activity*, the flow of thoughts. Over the days, I discovered that by slowing one activity, the other activity also slowed down. This morning, when I was totally relaxed and calm, I cannot even say that I did anything, but all activity stopped. What remained was the witness, who was only aware of the stillness. This stillness dissolved even the witness, to leave behind a nameless consciousness. There was no description, and the words failed." Sopān was beside himself with ecstasy.

Nivṛttināth hugged him and spread his arms to include Jñānā and Muktāyi in that embrace, unifying them. A little later, he spoke and there was that joy of accomplishment, of completing a task and of fulfilling a mission: "We are blessed because of the virtues accrued by our parents and ancestors, which has brought this understanding of this great Truth, in this very life with little effort and short time. People take many lives to do so. Come inside the hut; let us take the blessings of our *Bāpa*Viṭṭhalu *and* Rakhumāyi!"

When they stood before the idols they had worshipped since their childhood, it felt as if the images of their favourite deities had come alive, happy that their children were with them, all graceful help would be available to them and that they were now ready to take up the next task before them!

They heard someone call: "Nivṛttidādā, Jñānadev, where are you?"

It was Namu. They all felt grateful to the gods in front of them and fell prostrate in veneration. Coming out, they saw their sister Namu beaming, as she carried their food. Jñānadev, however, felt that it had something more than just affection of a mother ready to feed her children. So, he asked: "Namutāyi, do you have any message for us?"

She laughed and exclaimed: "Jñānadev, nothing can be

hidden from you! Yes, my brothers and little sister. I do have very good news for you. It appears all your sufferings will be over soon." Then she narrated what had happened.

That morning, Namu had seen a motherless litter of puppies. She had searched for the mother, but a boy had told her that the mother had died and had been buried. Unable to bear the plight of the puppies, which had not even opened their eyes, she thought of taking them home. However, knowing the violent nature of her father, Visobāpant, she took them to Gangādhar Śāstry who was quite fond of her. Seeing the orphaned pups, he started feeding them with milk. While he was appreciating her compassionate nature, she asked him if people could be compassionate on these pups. "Why we are so harsh on the orphaned human children?"

When he enquired about the children, she told, about the children of Viṭṭhalpant and Rukmiṇidevi. He realised the folly of the decision of cruel *dharma sabhā* of which he too was a member. He told Namu that though he could not possibly reverse the decision, he could give a letter of recommendation to Vidyādhar Śāstry, who was a respectable member of Paiṭhaṇ *dharma sabhā*, which was above all and had a powerful influence on the local *sabhās,* who will prevail upon the *sabhā* to issue a *Śuddhipatra*, a letter of absolution.

Concluding her narration, Namu continued with joy: "Enough have you suffered, my dear brothers and sister. Make preparations to go to Paiṭhaṇ forthwith. When you get the *śuddhipatra*, you will be rightfully welcomed into the society."

While all other siblings were happy, Nivṛttināth was silent for a while and then said gravely: "Tell me, why do we require *śuddhipatra* from those who themselves are not *Śuddha*, pure? Namu, we have all been accepted by God and there is no need for society's permission."

There was silence for a while, and then Jñānadev approached Nivṛttināth and said softly: "Gurudev, we are still living in this society and if we have to spread spirituality, we need their approval. Who knows *Dādā*, there may be some positive outcome from our visit to Paiṭhaṇ."

"Jñānā, if you say so, I will accompany you all to the end of the world!"

Jñānadev added with his tongue in cheek: "Gurudev, we want you to be with us to enter the world!"

They all laughed. The Quartet was ready to take on the world!

□

6
Affirmation and Acceptance

A soft breeze blowing from the valley below was so refreshing that they soon recovered from the journey on foot. The graceful flow of River Godāvari was pleasing to the eye. The majestic tower of Ekalingeśwar temple dominated the town of Paiṭhan. It had been a long tiresome walk for Sopān and Muktāyi, but all along Nivṛttināth's narration of experiences with his *guru*, Gahininàth, as well as Jñānadev's sweet and meaningful *abhaṅgs* had eased their strain. People on way, especially the farmers, had open heartedly given them food. And presently, they had their destination in sight, filling their hearts with hope.

Though Paiṭhan was associated with Sanskrit scholarship and considered to be a haven of learning, it was now a place for hair-splitting arguments and fanaticism. These thoughts were going on in the mind of Nivṛttināth, when he heard Jñānadev, who got up first and said: "*Dādā*, Sopān, Muktāyi, come let us enter the town!" Nivṛttināth responded: "*Alak Niraṅjan*!" Strange as it may seem but with that, all of them were enthused and filled with vigour. Muktāyi walked in front, Jñānadev in the middle, Nivṛttināth and Sopān in the back.

As they passed through the farmlands, the farmers living in their huts nearby, though curious, were warm in welcoming the bright children by offering them jaggery and water, which they had happily accepted. Then they started walking towards the town. The near outskirts were occupied by the tradesmen, like smiths, masons, carpenters and the like. And finally, they entered Paiṭhan.

Like most of the towns, it had developed around the temple of Ekalingeśwar; residences of *pundits* and *purohits* occupied the places nearest to the temple, then came the market place. The Quartet approached the temple and sat on the steps. All the eyes were on them and a few Brahmins came near them to know their identity. A young *vaṭu*, the apprentice priest, spoke: "Where are you from?"

Jñānadev stood and after saluting the priest, responded: "We have come from Āḷandi and are being sent by Gangādhar Śāstriji. Can you please direct us to Vidyādhar Śāstriji?"

Impressed by the humility of the boy, he said: "I am Goviṅdpanth, and shall gladly take you to him. But first you must come to my house and have some refreshments. My mother will be very pleased to meet you, as she is from Āḷandi. She would love to learn the developments in Āḷandi!"

When they reached the house of Goviṅdpanth, his mother Bhāmātāi, came rushing out as soon as she heard the word, 'Āḷandi'! Somehow, they all were reminded of their own mother. She asked them to come near and held Muktāyi close, as she asked:"Children, from which family are you, and what about your parents?"

There was concern in her voice. Apparently, she felt that something was seriously wrong and these children needed all the help they needed. Jñānadev, touched by her feelings, responded matching his concern with hers: "Viṭṭhalpant and Rukmiṇidevi were our parents."

Bhāmātāi broke down. The children and also Goviṅda were surprised at her reaction. After recovering, she said, wiping the tears off with the edge of her sari: "Rukmiṇi was my childhood friend and we were neighbours. I had known her very well and was with her when she had conversation with Swāmi Rāmānanda. Just before your father's return to

Āḷandi, I got married and came here. I have been receiving the news from time to time. I wanted to help you all along. The children of my intimate friend are my own children." She pressed Muktāyi to her bosom.

After the refreshments, Govind took them to the temple of Ekalingeśwar where the *dharma sabhā* was to meet. As they waited for the members headed by Vidyādhar Śāstri in the precincts of the temple, the devotees as well as the priests were attracted to the bright faces and noble bearing. Their calm and graceful presence could not be ignored.

Curious as most people are, they had heard about the four children from Āḷandi and waited to see the outcome, at the *sabhā*. Soon the scholars arrived, headed by Vidyādhar Śāstri. Govind approached the raised seat and handed over the letter from Gangādhar Śāstri. After opening the letter and going through its contents he said gravely: "We have heard of a *sannyāsi* returning to *gṛhastāśrama*. I request all of you to refer to the sacred texts of *Dharmaśāstra* to find out whether there is any way to award *śuddhipatra* to his offspring."

All eyes turned to the Quartet. There was affectionate concern and also silent prayer in many hearts. But from among the scholars, there was only a cold and covert violence in their look. Nivṛttināth, however, was certain of their verdict, but he was also amused at the outcome of this memorable meeting – memorable because the whole region would know of the grace of God over the Quartet!

Hours later, every single scholar declared that there was no mercy for a *sannyāsi* who had abandoned his higher *aśrama* to accept a lower one. There had been no other solution for his offspring than to be excommunicated from the society. Vidyādhar Śāstri declared gravely, looking at Jñānadev: "Gangādhar has been my *gurubhāi*, brother disciple. But we are helpless and cannot possibly issue any *śuddhipatra*. The sacred canon does not allow any digression."

Jñānadev responded in all humility but firmness: "I salute all the wise *pundits* adorning this *sabhā*. I am Jñānadev. But will you please forgive me if I express a small doubt?"

When Vidyādhar nodded affirmatively, he continued: "Our spiritual texts, like the *Upaniṣads* and *Śrīmad Bhagavad Gītā* declare that it is the same Lord, who occupies the heart of every *sthāvaram*, inanimate thing and *jangamam*, conscious being, and also that, seeking God and realising Him is its birthright. Why can't this *dharma sabhā* follow the declaration of the *Śāstras*, spiritual texts which are meant to take all of us towards *mokṣa*?"

With that there was a furore in the *sabhā*, but there were also, some nodding and appreciating heads. The people who had come there out of curiosity, however, were in agreement with this child.

One could see that most members of the *sabhā* were annoyed with this little boy for challenging their verdict! Vidyādhar felt that it was a personal insult to him. With his face red with anger, he asked: "You have the cheek to challenge the verdict of this sacred *dharma sabhā*? We are the custodians of *dharma* and will never allow any wrongdoing people to flout age-old laws."

Jñānadev, calm and composed, replied calmly and in all humility: "Mahārāj, I am not challenging the role of *dharma sabhās* in maintaining the law and order in the society. My humble appeal is not to restrict the sincere seekers in approaching our all-encompassing *adhyātma vidyā Śāstras*, spiritual texts, to realise the Truth enshrined in them. Your *śuddhipatra* will permit us to get initiated into *brahmacarya.* The experiential declarations roar that '*sarvam khalu idam Brahma*, verily All this is Brahma. This means living and non-living, which in essence means that there is nothing beyond Brahma."

Vidyādhar Śāstri flared up and shouted: "Do you mean to say that there is no difference between you and say, the buffalo which we see outside and both have the same consciousness?"

Jñānadev without losing his poise smilingly replied: "Yes Mahārāj, we are the same within; only our form is different."

With a sneer, he asked his attendant to bring the buffalo inside. When it was brought, he asked with a sneer: "What is his name?"

To which, the person accompanying the animal said: "Mahārāj, it is Jñānā!"

At this the assembly laughed as it matched with the name of the challenger! Vidyādhar asked Jñānadev mockingly: "So, his name also matches with yours! Can you make the buffalo chant the *Veda*?"

Jñānadev looked at his *guru*, Nivṛttināth, who just put his palm on his shoulder encouragingly. Jñānadev along with his siblings started walking towards the buffalo; the assembly followed, with Vidyādhar in the lead. The people as well as some members who had taken a liking towards this Quartet were very concerned about the outcome of this open and almost impossible challenge. Jñānadev fell at the feet of his *guru*, then went near the animal, caressed its head and then closed his eyes. A gruff voice was heard which recited the *mantra* with proper cadence:

'May my speech be firmly held in my mind,
May my mind be firmly held in my speech.
O Thou who art Manifestation be manifest unto me!
Guarding my knowledge like a lynch pin of the wheel,
Do not let the Truth taught to my ear, fall away!
By this wisdom that I learn,
I shall firmly, hold the days and the nights.
I will utter the Reality; I will utter the Truth.
May that nourish me, may that nourish the teacher.
May that nourish me, may That nourish the teacher.
Let the Peace descend on all three planes. AUM.'[31]

---

31. ॐ वाङ्मे मनसि प्रतिष्ठिता मनो मे वाचि प्रतिष्ठितम्। आविराविर्म एधि।
वेदस्य म आणीस्थः श्रुतं मे मा प्रहासीः।
अनेनाधी नेनाहोरात्रान्सन्दधामि ऋतं वदिष्यामि। सत्यं वदिष्यामि। तन्मामवतु। तद्वक्तारमवतु।
अवतु मां अवतु वक्तारमवतुवक्तारम्।
।। ॐ शान्तिः शान्तिः शान्तिः ।। ऋग्वेदः ।।

The whole assembly was nonplussed! How was it possible? And yet the child had stood with his eyes closed and hands folded in veneration. They noticed that the aura around him was so explicit that it could be felt by all of them. Immediately, the whole mood inside the temple transformed into one of devotion and celebration.

The first person to fall at the feet of Jñānadev was Vidyādhar Śāstri, who spoke with his tearful eyes and voice choked with genuine emotion: "Forgive me, Jñānadev, forgive me! Unaware that I was of your spiritual achievement, I passed a verdict. You made the buffalo chant the most relevant *maṅtra* which we all should know!"

Jñānadev too was surprised at this turn of events! But he once again fell at the feet of Nivṛttināth. One person very keenly observing this whole episode was Goviṅda. When the buffalo was chanting the *Veda*, his eyes were on the Quartet. He saw that while Jñānadev, Sopān and Muktāyi stood with their eyes closed in deep prayer, Nivṛttināth was gazing at Jñānadev as if giving him all the power. He was touched by the unity and intimacy of these brothers and sister. Instead of weakening them, the struggle so far had only strengthened them. He decided that he would follow them and try to serve them in whatever capacity he could.

Meanwhile Vidyādhar lifted Jñānadev and took him to the dais. He wrote with his own hand a letter, which in spirit, mentioned that it was foolish and downright impertinent to issue *śuddhipatra* to these children who were themselves so pure that they purified the vision and attitude of the *impure dharma sabhā*; that it was as ludicrous to give permission to the Sun to shine, to the water to flow and air to blow; that the whole *dharma sabhā* had unanimously agreed that these guileless and godly children had much to offer to the society.

When they returned to Govinda's house, Bhāmātāi hugged them with tears of joy. She said with all the sincerity and seriousness: "My children, you can stay here with us. Why do you have to return to the town where you are being insulted and persecuted? Our Govinda will have noble company, and he too shall imbibe some things from your life."

Jñānadev said with all affection: "*Āyi*, we are blessed to have come here and get your affection. We shall come here again sometime in future. But now we must return to Āḷandi, to revive the status of our dear parents, who sacrificed their lives for our welfare and vindicate their reputation."

Bhāmātāi however said: "Jñāna *Bāl*, child, at least stay tonight and have your food from my hand!"

She dragged Muktāyi near her, who said innocently: "*Dādā*, it has been a very long time since we had food from *Āyi's* hands."

Next day when the Quartet began its return journey, Goviṅda expressed his wish to accompany them. Nivṛttināth assured him that he could join them at a proper time. For the present, his presence was necessary at home with his parents. Happy that the events had happened in their favour, they retraced their steps in all enthusiasm. Muktāyi sang and danced, rehearsing the *yajñopavītam*, thread ceremony and how she would be the first to give all of her brothers their first *bhikṣā*!

The news travelled faster than the children. Many were quite happy that the children of Viṭṭhalpant and Rukmiṇidevi would at last find their rightful place in the society. Most of all, Sītābāī, her friends and her daughter Namu were literally dancing in their mind. However, the members of *dharma sabhā*, especially Visobāpant was extremely angry and bitter on Paiṭhan *sabhā*. He started talking against them, accusing them of easily falling prey to miracles!

It was forenoon when Nivṛttināth, Jñānadev, Sopān and Muktāyi reached Āḷandi after ten days. First, they all approached Indrāyaṇi Māyi and expressed their gratitude. After their bath, they proceeded to Siddheśwara temple to have *darśana* of Lord Siddheśwara and hand over the *śuddhipatra* to the *dharma sabhā*. They noticed that the crowd had already gathered and was waiting for them. Gangādhar

Śāstri came out and met them with so much affection that the children reciprocated by falling at his feet in gratefulness. He said happily: "*Bāḷāno*, children, I am so happy that you went to Paiṭhan. Come, I shall take you to the *sabhā*." After having the *darśana* of Lord Siddheśwara, they proceeded to the hall filled with scholars and onlookers. Jñānadev approached the head of the *sabhā* and handed the letter from Vidyādhar Śāstri. After going through the contents, the head looked at Visobā, who nodded his head to proceed with the announcement.

Clearing his throat, he said contemptuously: "It appears that the sin has become stronger than *dharma.* It is unbelievable that Paiṭhan *sabh*ā, which used to be in our highest esteem, too has fallen! They got carried away by the miracle these sinful children performed there. Moreover, they themselves agree that they are incapable of giving any *śuddhipatra*! No wonder *Kaliyuga* is in ascendance! I have no further remarks to make except that they cannot possibly stay even on the outskirts of Āḷandi."

So saying he got up from his seat and walked out arrogantly, followed by Visobā and others. But Gangādhar Śāstri was totally flabbergasted by the behaviour of the *sabhā* of which he too was a member. Jñānadev was nonplussed and sat on the floor of the temple, leaning on a pillar. There were tears in his eyes, and pain in his heart. Nivṛttināth approached him and started caressing his back, while Sopān and Muktāyi came and sat near him in support.

Gangādhar, it appeared, was the most disturbed of the lot who said throat choked with emotion: "Forgive me *bāḷāno,* I never knew that our *sabhā* is so fanatic and narrow to misunderstand and misinterpret the spirit of the letter written by Vidyādhar. It certainly is a bane of the people of Āḷandi and of this region."

Silently stood Namu, shedding tears, for she knew that it was her father who had turned the tables.

They saw that there was no point in staying any more even in the outskirts, as they had been banished from this region, Jñānadev, Sopān and Muktāyi walked in all sadness and wondering at the outcome of their apparently useless effort. Nivṛttināth, however, walked steadily behind Jñānadev with a composed mind. There was no doubt whatsoever in his mind that every event had the will of Providence behind it. Moreover, he was convinced that the time was more than ripe for him to pass on another insight he had at Siddheśwara temple. Jñānadev stopped for a while and turned towards a tree alongside the rubble path they were walking, and sat facing the sunset.

Nivṛttināth went and sat beside him while the younger siblings sat at a distance. Jñānadev turned towards his brother and said: "*Dādā*, you were so right when you had said that the *śuddhipatra* received from those who themselves need purification is useless. I now feel that we better retreat to a secluded place and continue our *sādhanā* and move towards our own salvation."

Nivṛttināth smiled and said with lot of affection and conviction: "No Jñānā, the other day, you were right in convincing me! We are living in a society which has strayed away from the Māṇus *dharma*. It needs direction urgently, like fish needing water, or a drowning man needing air to breathe. If persons like us start looking in other direction and seek our own personal salvation, then who will care for the society?"

Jñānadev said impatiently: "But don't you see *Dādā*, the society does not need us; it has banished us from their very sight."

Understanding fully his feelings, Nivṛttināth responded after a pause: "It is true that a certain group has turned us away, but there are wonderful people out there: the simple, pure and innocent people who can feel, and are themselves facing vicissitudes and problems even to survive. Never have they made any complaints about life; instead, they extend their help to one and all. Many times, we even see that they are more satisfied than our so-called scholars."

Jñānadev thought awhile, and he saw that his *guru* was

right. He remembered that even in Āḷandi, there were his foster mothers and sisters. Not all persons were cruel and heartless. A thought arose in his mind, reminding him of the affection they had received on way to Paiṭhan and back. He responded enthusiastically: "Gurudev, I am able to clearly see now, what you are trying to tell me is that we can perform our *sādhanā* while spreading the Māṇus *dharma*!"

Nivṛttināth patted him on his back and said encouragingly: "Yes Jñānā, all our effort should be, to be the living examples of Māṇus *dharma*. Then we need not go to the society, but the society will come to us! But presently, we have to reach some village before the nightfall."

When they started walking again, their spirits were lifted, to face life. They heard the jingle of bells from behind. It was a farmer hurrying towards his home on his bullock cart. The jingles came from the small bells adorning the necks of the two handsome animals. It appeared they were well looked after. Seeing the children alone, he slowed down and asked: "Where are you going *porāno*, children? You look tired and do not even have any footwear."

Jñānadev replied with a smile: "*Kākā*[32] we really do not know where God is taking us."

The farmer said with concern: "You appear to be Brahmin children."

Jñānadev responded with a tinge of humour: "*Kākā,* we were definitely born in a Brahmin family, but we do not have any caste since we are excommunicated!"

The farmer felt compassionate and added spontaneously: "O my God! Stop walking." So saying, he got down from his cart and lifted Muktāyi and made her sit, and then helped the three brothers climb the cart. He said in all affection: "Don't worry! From now on, you will stay with me and give company to my own children. We will share whatever food we have and be happy."

Jñānadev was touched by the spontaneous love and

32. It means 'uncle' in Marathi language.

concern shown by *Kākā*. Looking at his *guru* he smiled. In that smile he conveyed that already there are many persons following Māṇus *dharma*.

Later when the two younger siblings retired for the night, the two elder brothers sat under a tree, enjoying the moonlit night. Jñānadev had regained his composure. Nivṛttināth slowly started speaking and in the background were the sounds of the night: "Jñānā, let me ask you one question: why do you think that life is testing us by presenting new challenges at every turn?"

Jñānadev pondered for a while before responding: "Gurudev, I feel they are thrown as opportunities for us to be strong as God has some important work for us. The more important the work, the more strength we need!"

Nivṛttināth smiled and said encouragingly: "You are right! The task before us is really big and we need all the strength. I have been noticing that out of all the problems we have been facing, the insult meted out to us appears to disturb you the most. Why do you think it is so?"

Though Jñānadev was aware of his reactions to insults, he did not expect to face this question from his *guru* who was his own elder brother! He thought that his reactions to insults was very natural because he felt, and that too because of his sensitive heart. He answered hesitantly as he knew that the question had a deeper purpose: "Gurudev, it may be due to my deep sensitivity and as you had told me that I am very emotional."

Nivṛttināth knew that the time was ripe for him to give the real cause behind all those insults and his reactions to them: "Jñānā, the events have a very great purpose in preparing you for the task ahead."

As he uttered this sentence, everything around became silent, as if eager to listen. Jñānadev became extremely awake and alert. "Jñānā, you have been experiencing that God dwells in all beings, which made the buffalo chant the Veda. But when you say all, you have not yet included those beings who insult you, who keep on giving you pain! The repeated incidents that you undergo, or for that matter anyone undergoes, is to teach you that your ego is nothing in comparison with God. The day you see that it is God alone who is with you in the form of animals, human beings, friends as well as foes, and material things, you become a perfect instrument for God to work through you."

Jñānadev's being was filled with his master's words till they entered each pore and cell and he was blessed with an experiential understanding. Nivṛttināth knew that Jñānadev too knew!

Morning brought new light and lightness to Jñānadev. The change was observed by Muktāyi. Her heart filled with pride, hugged her dear brother.

"Come children for food!" It was *Kākā* calling out. He had brought *poḷis*[33] and some vegetables. He said he was going for water to a nearby well. When they started eating just after the first morsel, Muktāyi felt very thirsty and asked for water. Jñānadev saw a water source in the opposite side of the road, so he took her to it. After clearing the water, he made her drink. In the meantime, a few villagers, curious to know what the youngsters were up to, started shouting to not drink the water as the water source was haunted and not at all potable. But the brother and the sister had already drunk from the well! Worried and afraid lest something untoward were to befall the children, *Kākā* came rushing. But to his consternation, he found them safe and sound! He blurted: "*Devā*re *Deva*, I had gone to get you safe water, why did you drink this water?"

"Why *Kākā*, what is wrong with this water?" Jñānadev asked to which *Kākā* said: "This *bāvḍi* is haunted; whoever drinks from it they enter into his body."

Jñānadev said: "Both Muktāyi and I have drunk from it, but nothing has happened, and nothing will happen to us. You too start using the water from this *bāvḍi;* nothing will happen." So, saying he offered some water to *Kākā* who drank

33. In Maharashtra, *roṭis* are called as *poḷis.*

it. When nothing happened, he encouraged everyone else to drink. They all followed and were convinced Jñānadev was God! He only smiled and declared: "Each one of you is God! He is in everyone and everything, from the ant to the mountain. Nobody can ever harm God! Discover that God within you as well as outside you."

Someone from the crowd asked: "*Devā*, but how can we discover?"

Jñānadev replied: "Together we shall learn!"

And so started the journey of acceptance of God!

□

7
The Alchemy

'O mind, hold firmly the essential Truth through Divine name.
Hari the Lord will shower His grace upon you.
It is so easy to repeat His name: Rāmakṛṣṇa Goviṅda.
Repeat it always with all your being.
There is no other truth than God's name.
To walk other path without the name is just a waste of time.
Jñānadev says silently behold the Japamāḷā that is inside you.
And repeat the name of God unceasingly.'[34]

It was twilight when Jñānadev had started singing the *abhaṅg.* Jñānadev sat under a tree, with Nivrttināth on his right, Muktāyi and Sopān on his left. The crowd was repeating the refrain, '*Rāma Kṛṣṇa Goviṅda*' swaying to the rhythm of the *abhaṅg*. There was joy, celebration in an overall milieu of holiness. They really felt that he was making them walk the path of *bhakti* by holding their hand. The holy atmosphere created had dissolved all their so-called problems in the chanting. The strain of walking long distances for drinking

---

34. एक तत्त्व नाम दृढ धरि मना। हरीसि करूणा येईल तूझी।। १।।
तें नाम सोपेरें रामकृष्ण गोविंद। वाचेसी सद्गद जपें आर्धीं।। २।।
नामा परतें तत्त्व नाही रे अन्यथा। वाया आणिका पंथा वरी जासी झणें।। ३।।
ज्ञानदेवा मौन जपमाळा अंतरी। धरोनि श्रीहरि जपे सदा।। ४।।

water had been eliminated. They felt genuine love and respect for the Quartet as, for most of them, the children had become their own! Though *Kākā* had felt a pride when he had brought these wonderful children with him due to some strong bond with them, this was something different, which he had never experienced before. When the euphoria was over, an old farmer asked: "*Bāḷ*, why is it that by just taking the name of God, all of us are feeling so happy?"

Jñānadev looked at his master, offered his *praṇām* to take his permission, and then replied with a smile: "You have just answered your own question!" When everyone wondered what he meant by that, he continued: "You said just by taking the name, it means that there was neither any desire, nor was there any effort on anyone's part. It was spontaneous and effortless. All of you work throughout the day. How do you perform any work?"

There was silence for some time, when a youth stood up and said: "We do any work because we want something from that work. We work in the field because we want to grow food-grains."

Jñānadev continued happily: "Yes, we need something, because of which there is effort in our work, not only physical, but more so mental effort, as there are thoughts of concern whether the climate will be good or worries like, 'will it be sufficient for our landlord's as well as our own needs?' But when we sang the Lord's name, neither was there effort nor any mental strain.

"Moreover, during our singing, none of us was even conscious that we are singing! And there was only the *abhaṅg*! While in such singing, there is no *separation of 'I-we-are-singing'.* That is why it is called *abhaṅg*, undivided! There is no division between the song and the singer."

Some people were able to understand what Jñānadev was trying to say. For the rest, it was a wonderful experience, which should be repeated time and again! Conscious of their pulse, Jñānadev continued: "If this repetition of God's name has given you joy and peace, it is more than enough. We will meet every evening here. Now please return to your homes and keep performing your duties to fulfil the responsibilities. All your responsibilities and the works have been allotted to you by God. This means, that you are really doing the Lord's work. If you keep repeating 'Rāmakṛṣṇa Goviṅda', you will be remembering that you are His servant, and are doing His work."

Nivṛttināth was blissful at the turn of events or Jñānadev's fruitful interaction with the simple villagers. For them, repetition of the name alone was sufficient to travel the path of spirituality. However, Jñānadev had to also include others, specially thinking people. So, he called Jñānadev one morning and asked: "Jñānā, that evening when you were talking to the people, you said that it was more than enough to just repeat the name, the rest will be taken care of by God. Can you tell me how?"

Jñānadev knew that his *guru* wanted him to give more thought to his suggestion, so that it could be explained. He replied after a pause: "Gurudev, the persons who have given us shelter here, are all very pure and simple, without any cleverness or ego. For them, the *nāma,* name, is *nāva,* the boat to take them across the *bhavasāgar*, the ocean of indulgence and involvement. But the persons, who do not have purity and simplicity as their virtues, will have to be taught something more to purify the mind and heart. I have been thinking about it. Can you please guide me?"

"Jñānā, *tapas* is the only guidance! You take a further plunge inside and discover the source of all thought and feelings. It would be better if you discover it on your own." So said Nivṛttināth and closed his eyes, to indicate that he was done with talking.

After falling prostrate, Jñānadev withdrew towards River Bāṇagaṅgā and selected a shady tree that was on a raised spot overlooking the river as well as the agricultural land. The farmers were sowing seeds in the tilled land. Jñānadev too was ready with the seed of contemplation in his alert mind. The seed had been sown by his *guru,* Nivṛttināth! Just then he heard the distant voice of the farmer who sang: "*Eka tattva nāma, dṛḍha dhari manā...Rāmakṛṣṇa Goviṅda!*"

The others joined the chorus: "*Rāmakṛṣṇa Goviṅda... Rāmakṛṣṇa Goviṅda...*!!"

This was a strong suggestion for Jñānadev to plunge within.

As he directed the attention within, his first encounter was with the *manas,* that function of the mind which collects the information gathered by the five senses outside. It is necessarily random as its function is to gather the information of the changing world outside. He withdrew his participation by not reacting to the senses information which helped him to silence the *manas*. By refraining from judging them as good or bad, the *buddhi*, the function of *antaḥkaraṇa*, the mind stuff, which analyses, decides and judges, became silent. He became aware of another facet called *cittam*, the function of remembering, the storehouse of all impressions and experiences, his knowledge and wisdom. Just then, his attention started getting stuck to those experiences that had pained him and his family. He realised that they were still lingering because he had reacted during or immediately after the experience! With awareness, he proceeded further within to become aware of the entity behind all these functions of *antaḥkaraṇa – ahaṅkāra*. When he refused to pay attention to it, there was total silence!

When Jñānadev opened his eyes there was an explosion of joy. He realised that it was nearing twilight; he got up and with that same joy,started walking towards the place of gathering for *nāmasmaraṇam*, the chanting and remembering the name.

When the *guru* and his disciple met the next day, Jñānadev shared his experiential insight, describing every little detail. Nivṛttināth said with satisfaction: "Good Jñānā, you have to go forward, do not stop! Go deeper, continue the *tapas*!"

Jñānadev understood and proceeded to the same tree,

where he found Sopān in deep meditation. He knew that Sopān had really mastered the art of meditation and was happy that he could benefit from the company of his younger brother. Jñānadev sat next to him. Almost immediately his *antaḥkaraṇa* delved within to stand witness to *ahaṅkāra*. It was then that Jñānadev became aware of the *prāṇa*, the vital force behind all activity – physical, mental, intellectual, as well as emotional. It struck him that all these activities had only a single source in *prajñā,* consciousness. After awhile, Jñānadev opened his eyes to see Sopān, who looked at him with affection to say: "*Dādā*, you came and sat near me and that was why the meditation was really deep. I learnt a few things today." So, saying, he got up and prostrated.

Jñānadev got up and held his dear brother close and said: "Sopān, my dear brother, by sitting next to you, I have learnt something very important today. I must thank you for it!"

Sopān was confused as to why was *Dādā* thanking him? As if reading his mind, Jñānadev responded: "Brother, your meditation helped me to plunge easily within, to understand the inner workings much better. What did you learn Sopān?"

"*Dādā*, it is easier to control the gross instruments through subtler instruments, and everything comes under our control when we identify with *prajñā*!"

At this Jñānadev was extremely happy. He expressed it through his hearty laughter. When they started to return, he said patting the back of Sopān: "Sopān, Lord Kṛṣṇa says, in the *Bhagavad Gītā*, 'The senses are subtler than the body; deeper than the senses is the *manas*; *buddhi* is subtler than the *manas*; and greater than the *buddhi* is He (the self).'[35] As I was next to you, I too learnt this great Truth. It helped me to get an idea of controlling our lower emotions. I will do further *tapas* and learn more through my own experience."

Just then they heard Muktāyi calling them. Her tone was that of a mother trying to admonish her children for being late for the food: "Control is possible only when you have sufficient

35. इन्द्रियाणि पराण्याहुरिन्द्रियेभ्यः परं मनः। मनसस्तु परा बुद्धिर्यो बुद्धे परसस्तु सः।। ३.४२।।

energy. How will you have it when you are so forgetful about food?! Come soon, Nivṛttidādā is waiting."

When they reached the temple, their *guru* was beaming, for he had known about the experience of his brothers. When they looked into his brilliant eyes, they too knew *that He knew*!

'With attributes as well as being without attributes are wonderful;
This Viṭṭhala is the eternal Brahman.
He is the captivator of mind, saviour of the downtrodden;
This Viṭṭhala is the eternal Brahman.
The meditated, meditator, meditation, is unblemished mind;
This Viṭṭhala is the eternal Brahman.
Jñānadev sings songs on bliss;
This Viṭṭhala is the eternal Brahman.'[36]

Jñānadev's voice was like honey to the ears of the listeners. The farmer-folk and the workers did not bother about the meaning of the *abhaṅg*. But yes, they felt its mood well, so well that there were many with tears of joy and choked throats! Then in that mood of euphoria they started singing '*Rāmakṛṣṇa Goviṅda*' followed by '*Jai Jai Rāmakṛṣṇa Hari*'. Both Nivṛttināth and Jñānadev were totally convinced that for the simple folk, just the act of *nāmasmaraṇam* was more than enough! They were really blessed indeed. The Quartet joined the celebration of ecstasy with these people who had accepted them as their very own, right from their first day in this village.

All the participants of this festival of bliss had repaired to their homes, when silence descended on the Quartet and they experienced an intimate oneness that was beyond words!

At this point of time, within the heart of Jñānadev an insightful feeling was evoked which brought a deeper understanding about the Quartet's so-called persecutors!

---

36. सगुण निर्गुण दोन्ही विलक्षण। ब्रह्म सनातन विट्ठल हा।। १।।
पतित पावन मानसमोहन। ब्रह्म सनातन विट्ठल हा।। २।।
ध्येय ध्यास ध्यान चित्त निरंजन। ब्रह्म सनातन विट्ठल हा।। ३।।
ज्ञानदेव म्हणे आनन्दाचे गान। ब्रह्म सनातन विट्ठल हा।। ४।।

Wanting to share this with others, Jñānadev opened his eyes to meet those of his preceptor. As if in expectation, Nivṛttināth asked eagerly:

"What is it Jñānā that you want to share?"

Jñānadev responded in joy: "Gurudev, a wonderful insight dawned on me. May I share it?"

"Of course, Jñāna...¯!"

Jñānadev started after much deliberation: "Gurudev, our so-called persecutors are actually suffering. They have the burden of their noble birth, of their scholarship and of their being holier than others! Their behaviour is like a child crying in pain when she or he steps on a thorny bush, or getting hurt while playing. We need to attend to their problems and relieve them of their burden."

Nivṛttināth was very happy on this noble development in his dear brother. He said heartily: "Jñānā, only now you can think of spreading Māṇus *Dharma*. As long as there is even a trace of bitterness for the so-called persecutors in the heart, you will not be able to live Māṇus *Dharma*, let alone spread it! Do you remember what I told you?"

Jñānadev replied, remembering: "Go forward, stop not! Continue the *tapas!*"

He had walked a distance when he reached the bank of Pravarā river, which was also called Amritavāhini. Jñānadev had not given any thought on his destination, but had allowed his legs to walk! But yes, his heart and mind were enveloped by the thought of reaching out to those whom he had once considered as adversaries! Though he had kept away from any negative reaction, he did have some pain over the turn of events. Now he knew that everything, every event and every being was there because he needed the experiences. Each of them had taught the Quartet some precious lesson that had made them what they were. The cool mild breeze made him aware of the water body, which turned out to be a river. He heard someone wish him: "*Rāmakṛṣṇa Goviṅda*!"

It was an old farmer Dhoṅḍu who had been a recent

addition to the *satsaṅga*. Jñānadev asked him: "*Kākā,* what is the name of this river?"

"*Devā*, she is now called as Pravarā, but her earlier name was Amritavāhini. After the *amṛta manthan*, churning of the ocean for elixir, it was on her banks that Lord Viṣṇu distributed it among gods and demons."

'How appropriate,' felt Jñānadev. The rain of *amṛta* is pouring in the *satsaṅga* and is being enjoyed by every person participating in it.

Dhoṅḍu continued: "*Devā*, after your arrival to this place, all our problems have been solved, and you and your brothers and sister have given us so much joy that we do not feel disturbed by anything! We do our work, chanting God's name and keep waiting for the evening *satsaṅga*. Come to my hut *Devā*, we all want to share a meal with you." He reached for Jñānadev's hand, holding it, started walking. Jñānadev remembered the grip of his revered father Viṭṭhalpant; with moist eyes he happily walked to the *bhākri* (dry *roṭis* of *jawār*, pearl millet) waiting for him! He discovered to his pleasant surprise that Dhoṅḍu had much more than food; it was affection, intimacy and love. He noticed that Dhoṅḍu's family consisted not only of his wife and children, but a pair of bullocks, a dog, a cat, few squirrels and a variety of birds, like crows, sparrows, bull-bulls, parrots! Each being was a respected member of this dear old farmer, who not only grew food, but was harvesting love!

Nivṛttināth noticed a welcome change in Jñānadev: every action of his was filled with love! It was not for anyone or anything in particular; it was love for the whole existence. The *satsaṅga* had only begun, the chorus chanting of '*Rāmakṛṣṇa Goviṅda*' and '*Jai Jai Rāmakṛṣṇa Hari*' was on, and the people were swaying to the rhythm. Jñānadev entered the place, his eyes were luminous – it felt as though he was seeing the Lord everywhere. His eyes met those of Nivṛttināth, his beloved *guru* and brother, and he fell prostrate.

Nivṛttināth blessed him by blissfully patting him on his back. He observed: "Jñānā, you have arrived! We are all blessed, my dear brother!"

Sopān and Muktāyi were all ecstatic with joy. Sopān was silent but Muktāyi asked mischievously: "Jñāna *Dādā*, it appears your being has received *puraṇpoḷi*".[37]

Jñānadev responded in kind, "Yes *Māyi*, I tasted *pūrṇa*[38] *poḷi* and you already know its taste!"

She laughed, while Nivṛttināth rejoined: "Jñānā, sing that *abhaṅg* you used to sing about chanting Hari through the mouth repeatedly, the acquired *puṇya* has no limit."

> '*All the four* Vedas *give the wisdom of Hari; the six* Śāstras *declare Hari is the origin of world. Eighteen* Purāṇas *sing His glories. Take the butter churned out of them to be Infinite Hari.*
>
> *Hari and the individual soul are the same; do not divert your mind on any other.*
>
> *Jñānadev says chanting Hari is Vaikuṅṭha; then we will see Hari within and without.*
>
> *Chant Hari through the mouth repeatedly, the acquired puṇya has no limit.*'[39]

Everyone joined the chorus '*Hari mukhe mhaṇā...*' and transcended their body-mind. The whole atmosphere was charged with holy vibrations and ecstasy. When the singing concluded and the people dispersed, Nivṛttināth came near Jñānadev and put his hand on his head to bless him. Jñānadev,

37. Marāṭhi delicacy—sweet *Roṭis* prepared out of flour, Jaggary and Bengal gram.

38. Fullness.

39. चहुं वेदी जाण साही शास्त्रीं कारण। अठराही पुराणे हरिसी गाता।। १।।
मंथुनी नवनीता तैसे घे अनंता। वाया व्यर्थ कथा सांडी मार्गु।। २।।
एक हरी आत्मा जीवशीव सम। वायां तू दुर्गमा न घाली मन।। ३।।
ज्ञनदेवा पाठ हरि हा वैकुंठ। भरला घनदाट हरि दीसे।। ४।।
हरी मुखे म्हणा हरी मुखे म्हणा। पुण्याची गणना कोण करी।।
This is the second of the twenty-seven *abhaṅgs* of *Haripāṭh*, repeated every evening by the *vārkari* tradition. The language besides being sweet is easy to understand.

in turn, bowed low at the feet of his *guru* in total surrender. The *guru* knew that his disciple was ready to spread Māṇus *Dharma*, well almost! There was only one, but a very important thing remained: to start writing about this Māṇus Dharma!

His Jñānā understood who said: "Gurudev with your grace that too shall be taken up! Before that, there are a few preparations for which I shall require some more time."

"Jñānā, I shall help you!"

Two more voices of Sopān and Muktāyi were heard: "We too shall!"

Sopān had always looked up to Jñānadev as his ideal. When he saw his ideal entering the *satsaṅga*, he knew that there was a transformation in his being. He was eager to learn what had transformed his dear *Dādā*!

It was late in the afternoon and Jñānadev was about to go out for a stroll. Sopān followed him and asked:"*Dādā,* can I come with you?"

Jñānadev responded: "Of course, Sopān, we will go near Amritavāhini river."

They started walking. Jñānadev knew that though his brother had some doubts, he was hesitant. And so, Jñānadev initiated the discussion: "Sopān, what is it that you want to know?"

With a sigh of relief, Sopān asked: "*Dādā*, that day you were away for the whole day, but when you returned in the evening for the *satsaṅga* there was a wonderful change in you, and ever since you appear different!"

Jñānadev laughed and said: "I am your same *Dādā*. But yes, Sopān my vision has changed. Ever since you were born, you know me to be very sensitive and emotional. I would get easily influenced and sometimes even disturbed by the events that shook our family. Tears were spontaneous for me, whether in joy or pain."

Sopān said in his brother's defence: "But *Dādā*, you are a poet, and are necessarily sensitive and emotional!"

Jñānadev was touched by Sopān's love for him. He said

amidst the ready tears that came out of his eyes: "Yes, my dear brother, I had always taken them to be a sign of weakness, and never knew that they are doorways to strength, joy and peace! That day I discovered my strength after meeting Dhoṅḍu, the farmer."

As usual Sopān's appetite to know more was aroused, so he responded: "*Dādā*, tell me more about it!"

Jñānadev looked around and continued after a pause: "Do you remember the time when we were forced out of Āḷaṅdi when they refused to even recognise the *śuddhipatra* given to us by Vidyādhar *Kākā*? I was almost shattered and wanted to retreat into wilderness for our own *mukti*. It was Nivṛtti *Dādā*, who said we must do something so that instead of our going to the people, the people will come to us. It was Gurudev's command and I willingly followed it. Then it struck me that my perception about our so-called persecutors was misdirected, and realised that they were actually suffering due to their perception of being high born, scholarly and holy – holier than others! This perception was weighing them down and was a burden upon their minds and as a reaction, they were misbehaving with others who were not like them!" Jñānadev paused for a while to look at the nature around.

"*Dādā*, then what happened?" Sopān asked in all eagerness.

Jñānadev laughed heartily. "Sopān, while I was near the river, I met Dhoṅḍu, the farmer. I was struck by his simplicity and purity of heart. He asked me...no, he took me by hand to his home for a meal. It was then that I noticed that here was a person who lived the essence of the verse from the *Bhagavad Gītā*: 'O Son of Pāṇḍu, he who works for my sake, depends on me, is devoted to me, has no attachment, and is free from malice towards all beings, reaches me.'[40] There is no one in this world, who is a stranger to him; everyone nay, every being is his friend. Whatever he has in his home, he shares with those who are near him. I had read this *Śloka* many times, but understood

---

40. मत्कर्मकृन्मत्परमो मद्भक्तः सङ्गवर्जितः। निर्वैरः सर्वभूतेषु यः स मामेति पाण्डवः।। ११.५५।।

its significance after being with Dhoṅḍu. It dawned on me and I realised once again that actually, there were no persecutors, and no victims! Every being and everything, including myself is just an instrument in the Lord's hands![41] My puniness, my pettiness and all the so-called bitter experiences just dissolved and my heart and mind became clear and pure."

There was silence and Sopān knew that his *Dādā* was re-living that experience. And in that mood, Jñānadev kept his hand on the head of Sopān. It was now his turn to be surprised and blissful and expansive and one with the whole Existence!

Sopān too realised when he returned to the so-called normal state, that what he had was not really an experiencer, for any experience requires *tripuṭi* – the experience, the experienced and experiencer. There was total identification with self, reality, Truth or whatever one may choose to call it! It was early evening and a parrot on a nearby Margosa tree was saying something in joy. Looking at it in all appreciation and love, Jñānadev said: "Sopān, my dear brother, I have understood what makes our hearts expansive! Whenever we feel empathetic to suffering of so-called others, our hearts go out to them. Actually, at that time the heart has identified with that person, it has melted or expanded, so much so that your eyes too start melting! Perhaps even the throat gets choked and the voice says, 'How unfortunate, poor man! Suppose, you are identified with the whole Existence, what will be your state of being?" Just by that suggestive question, Sopān was pushed back into himself!

Much later, when the sun had reached the western horizon, when the birds were returning to their nests, both the brothers came out to the external reality called the world. And Sopān did not find any difference between the inside and outside, between *sthāvaram* and *jangamam*!

In that very moment, Nivṛttināth was climbing the steps of the temple with Muktāyi behind him. He stopped and looked back at her. He was all smiles with bliss; she too responded

---

41. ईश्वरः सर्वभूतानां हृद्देशेर्जुन तिष्ठति। भ्रामयन्सर्वभूतानि यन्त्रारूढानि मायया।। १८.६१।।

in kind, and uttered in all joy: "*Dādā*, our dear brothers have arrived at *the temple*!"

The Quartet now had become the alchemists of emotions: of transforming base emotions like lust, anger, infatuation, greed, pride and jealousy into compassion, love and devotion. □

8
God's Friends

A tailor by profession, Dāmāśeṭi was extremely happy. His son had demanded a dress on his fifth birthday, not for himself, but for Viṭṭhala, the God of Pandharpur, the *Iśṭa* – the chosen deity of *vārkari sampradāya*. Being a *vārkari* himself, Dāmāśeti took it as a command of his chosen deity. Dāmāśeṭi's family was from Narasibāmaṇi and had been *vārkaris* for six generations. He remembered his own arrival at this sacred place. His father Hariśeṭi had never missed the *vāri*, the biannual sacred pilgrimage to Pandharpur in his life. In spite of his failing health, he took the pilgrimage and left his body as he prostrated in front of the idol of Viṭṭhala at Pandharpur. Since Dāmāśeṭi and Goṇāyi did not have any issues, they decided to shift from Narasibāmaṇi to Pandharpur. Their prayers were answered by Lord Viṭṭhala when they were blessed with a son Nāmdev, who was affectionately addressed by his parents and others as *Nāmā*. The first word Nāmā had uttered was *Viṭṭhala*! Dāmāśeṭi and Goṇāyi were convinced that Nāmā would fulfil the intense aspiration of their ancestors who had been *vārkaris* for generations – the vision of Viṭṭhala!

Nāmdev sat in front of the idol of Viṭṭhala after keeping the ornamental plate containing the noon food. His mother had told him that he should return home only after offering the food to the Lord. He noted that the food remained untouched.

So, he started talking to Viṭṭhala: "*Devā*, look what *Āyi* has prepared for you – dry vegetables, *poḷis, dālvaraṇ, kheē*r prepared from milk and butter."

There was no response from his Viṭṭhala. He once again coaxed him: "Viṭṭhala, I must tell you that I do not know any *maṅtras* to be chanted while offering *bhog*. *Bābā* has gone out of town; I will tell him to chant it. No, I have a better idea: I will learn the *maṅtras* from him after his return. Now do not be obstinate. Please start eating."

Again, seeing that there was no response, he said: "Viṭṭhala, I now remember, I did not close my eyes. Now I shall, but please eat."

Nāmā closed his eyes tightly. Opening only one eye, he peeped. No, He had not touched the food! This time he started crying and appealing amidst the tears and sighs: "Look, I have not eaten anything since morning, I am hungry. How can I eat if you do not start eating?" and started crying piteously and loudly!

Then he heard a sweet voice: "Nāmā, do not cry, I will eat!"

Nāmā's eyes closed in deep veneration. He kept repeating "Viṭṭhala ... Viṭṭhala' and lost the awareness of space and time! After a while, when he became aware of himself and space and time, his eyes fell on the idol of his God. It appeared as though it was smiling at him. And wonder of wonders, the lips were smeared with butter and milk! Just to assure himself, he looked at the plate of food. It was empty!

He danced and exclaimed: "Viṭṭhala, you ate the food I had brought! I did not know any *maṅtra*, nor did I know any ritual; all I know is how to call. Still, you ate the food? *Dhanya* am I." His throat choked with emotion and there were tears of joy.

The child had captured the heart of God! The purity, innocence and sincere call with real feeling had achieved what many had failed to, in spite of all their wisdom, their *tapas*, or their *bhakti*. Nāmā had achieved what his ancestors had craved for generations and his parents had prayed for, without any effort. It was his trust in his parents' words, which had made him to force Viṭṭhala into eating the food he had brought for his Lord!

When Nāmā entered home, Janā saw him in a mood of celebration. She was sweeping the courtyard. Janā was elder to him by six or seven years. She was an orphan, having lost both her parents and was of low birth. Dāmāśeti had found her on the steps of the temple of Pāṇḍuraṅga and had taken her under his care. He had felt that she would be an ideal companion for Nāmā. Instead, Janā had chosen to be Nāmā's servant, taking care of him. Seeing that the child's face lit from within, an ethereal smile adorning his lips, she asked: "Nāmā, what happened?"

Instead of replying to her question, he held her hands and started dancing! Joining him reluctantly, she repeated the question: "What is the occasion for this celebration, Nāmā?"

He replied in a shrill voice: "Janātāi, our Viṭṭhala ate the food I had offered."

Janā, knowing that Nāmā never lied, took him by his hand and made him sit on the verandah, asking him to tell everything. Nāmā narrated her, giving every little detail.

Janā's eyes were filled with tears of joy. Caressing his cheeks, she said: "*Dhanya* Nāmā, you are the beloved of our Viṭṭhala. Will you teach me how to call Him?"

"What is there, Janātāi? He is your own; call him, he will surely listen to you." So saying, Nāmā ran inside. His words 'He is your own' made a very deep impression her. Nāmā was right because for her, Viṭṭhala was her everything – father, mother, friend. What if her parents had passed away, He was there, and He will always be there! From that moment onwards, in all her activities, involved as she was doing all the chores in the house – cleaning utensils, washing clothes, husking grain, grinding flour, caring for cows, Janā started remembering Viṭṭhala and Nāmā had become her *guru*, and Janā his *śiśya,* disciple. Nāmā was her master and she considered herself to be his *dāsi*, servant.

Nāmdev's only interest was Viṭṭhala and his other

interests were Pāṇḍuraṅga, Kṛṣṇa, or Rukmiṇi! In other words, for him there was only God, Lord and nothing else. He would sit for hours in front of the image of the Lord and talk to God, play with the Lord. Many felt concerned about this abnormal behaviour. Some felt that he was mad! Of course, he was mad. We all are mad in a way – some of us for money, others for wife and children, and some others for name and fame! But what made Nāmā apart from others was that he was mad for God! He was a God's fool and God's friend!

His parents tried to coax him to take interest in their family trade of tailoring. They observed that God has given every one of us means like body and talents to feed ourselves and our family members. *Bhakti* is good as long as it is under control, like salt in food. Too much of it can be disturbing to the companions. Moreover, *bhakti* is not possible on an empty stomach! If there was any person who never lost faith in Nāmā, it was Janā, his disciple and servant. Janā always said that only Viṭṭhala is mandatory for life. Without Him, life is waste and meaningless!

'Living in Pandharpur, bathing in Caṅdrabhāgā;
And having the constant vision of Viṭhobā.
May these happen to me for life after life;
This is the only thing I ask of Śri Harī.
His name on lips always, the vision of saints,
And the feeling that this world itself is God.
Nāmā says let your eternal great gate,
Resound with the love filled kīrtan.'[42]

The residents of Pandharpur had started accepting Nāmdev's so-called abnormality! They had even started enjoying his *kīrtan satsaṅgas*. What he sang could be understood by all. His intense *bhāva,* feeling, could be felt by them. Like Janā, they felt that Viṭṭhala was not just an idol in

42. पंढरीचा वास चंद्रभागे स्नान। आणिक दर्शन विठोबाचे।। १।।
हेची घडो मज जन्मजन्मांतरी। मागणे श्रीहरी नाही दुजे।। २।।
मुखी नाम सदा संतांचे दर्शन। जनी जनार्दन ऐसा भाव।। ३।।
नामा म्हणे तुझे नित्य महाद्वारी। कीर्तन गजरी सप्रेमाचे।। ४।।

the temple, but someone very close to them. For the women-folk he was just a grown-up child! They felt that there was this same innocence, purity and simplicity of a child. Worldliness refused to even come near him! All he loved was his Viṭhobā and all he loved to do was his *kīrtan.* His parents were concerned about his survival in the world.

Seeing the parents worried one day, Janā assured them: "*Āyi, Bābā,* when Viṭṭhala is with Nāmā, why do you worry?"

Dāmāśeṭi felt reassured, but not Goṇāyi, who was irritated. She burst out: "Janā, it is because of your over-indulgence in him that Nāmā has become like this! Hereafter, stop talking to him."

Janā, in turn, responded with the patience of a mother: "*Āyi,* don't you remember my condition when I came to Pandharpur? I was taken in by you in your home. It was Nāmā who convinced me that Viṭṭhala is our own and that all you have to do is call him with all your heart and He will surely come! Nāmā is my *guru,* I will look after him."

Goṇāyi got more annoyed; she shouted: "What do you know of *bhakti,* an untouchable outcaste? You bother about your own duties of a maid-servant. That is what you will always be!"

Again, Janā responded with all affection: "*Āyi,* I am very happy and blessed to be the servant of this house. I shall always remain Nāmā's *dāsi.*"

Both Dāmāśeṭi and Goṇāyi were unaware of their house staging a wonderful spiritual play! While their son Nāmā was maturing into a Viṭṭhala *bhakta,* Janā had already an established companion of Viṭṭhala! Though Dāmāśeṭi had noticed the tremendous housework done by Janā, he had not bothered to know how she remained fresh and energetic throughout. But today, he had learnt more about his dear daughter: she was undisturbed at the reactions of Goṇāyi. On the contrary, she was composed, calm and blissful, giving them both assurances! How was it possible?

Just then, Nāmā returned home and sat near his father.

"Nāmā, your *Āyi* and I are concerned about you."

Nāmā smiled and responded: "But why are you concerned, *Bābā*?"

"We are alive today, but if you never think of earning your livelihood; what will happen?"

Nāmā replied spontaneously: "Viṭhobā is looking after the whole universe; are we not its very insignificant parts? He *was*, He *is* and He *will be*! Why should you or for that matter, anybody be concerned?"

In a trice, the son had put him at ease! But there was a matter he wanted to ask him. He said: "There is another matter, I want to know. From where does Janā derive her strength? And she claims you to be her *guru.*"

Nāmā laughed heartily and said, with tears of joy in his eyes: "*Bābā*, I am not her *guru*, I only told her that Viṭṭhala is our own and all you have to do is to call Him with all your heart. She is drawing all the energy and strength and joy and calmness and wisdom from her Viṭhobā! If she considers me as her *guru*, I am not responsible!" Smilingly he had come and laughingly Nāmā went out like a cool refreshing breeze in Dāmāśeṭi's summer of concern and worry.

Much earlier, one day, Janā, had *called* Viṭṭhala, with all her heart: "Nāmā told me that you would come. He said you are my own – father, mother, brother, sister and most intimate relation. Today I am tired; can't you come and help me with my duties? If I do not work for this family of mine, who will? I also know that it was you who gave me this family. Please come and help me. You are God, Lord of this universe. Can't you see that I am really in need of help? Please come Anaṅtā, Infinite!"

It was quite late in the night and she was grinding flour. As she turned the grindstone, she sang:

> '*While grinding and husking, I will sing on you O Anaṅtā.*
> *Never forgetting even for a moment, I will sing your name.*
> *Amidst all worldly activity, ever your name is on my lips.*
> *Mother, father, relative, sister, you are friend O Cakrapāṇi.*

The attention is on your feet, says dāsi of Nāmā.'[43]

Suddenly, Janā felt His presence, helping her turn the grindstone! The effort got evaporated and was replaced with joy and bliss! Janā, the servant, became the mistress of herself. Janā surrendered her everything – body, mind and heart at the feet of Viṭhobā, who was working through her!

Nāmā continued to do the only work he liked: singing the name of Viṭṭhala, Pāṇḍuraṅga and Viṭhobā! He would go to the temple and be there throughout the day and sometimes even nights. When asked how he could forget his parents and home, in turn he would ask them: 'How could anybody possibly forget Viṭṭhala after seeing Him but once!' He would repeatedly say that seeing the beauty of Viṭhobā, he never found any beauty anywhere else. His worldly interests had been totally replaced by his intense attachment to his Viṭṭhala! All his feelings, thoughts and his very soul were at HIS feet! He sang:

'My bhāva, feeling is towards your lotus feet.
Your form is ever in my eyes.
We discovered each other.
Never shall we separate for lives ahead.
You broke my illusion in attachment.
But I got attached to your feet!
You sent me away to transcendence of body.
But I put you in the prison of my heart!
Nāmā says, O dearest friend,
Tell me who tricked whom?'[44]

Both these devotees, who were brought together by Viṭhobā, befriended *Him* with their pure love and dedication. It was believed that Janā fed her Viṭhobā with her own hands,

43. दळिता कांडिता तुझ गाईन अनन्ता।। १।। नबिसंबे क्षणभरी। तुझ नाम गा मुरारी।। २।।
नित्य हाचि कारभार। मुखे हरी निरंतर।। ३।। मायबाप बंधू बहिणी। तू बा सखा चक्रपाणी।। ४।।
लक्षलागलें चरणासी । म्हणे नामयासी दासी।। ५।।

44. माझा भाव तुझे चरणी। तुझे रुप माझे नयनी।। १।। सापडलो एकामेकां। जन्मोजन्मी नोहे सुटका।। २।।
त्वां मोडिली माझी माया। मी तो जडलो तुझिया पायां।। ३।। त्वा मज मोकलिले विदेही।
मी तुज घातले हृदयी।। ४।। नामा म्हणे गा सुजाणा। सांग कोणे ठकविले कोणा ?।। ५।।

could even scold Him and God never left her, because she never left Him! And when Nāmā sang with *bhāva*, God danced to his tune! One friend was helped by God in doing all her worldly duties, who apparently did nothing herself. All the other friend did was to remember God or rather since Viṭhobā never left him, Nāmdev did not have to even remember Him, who did everything for him! Strange as it may seem, but they both sanctified holy Pandharpur.

Blessed were Dāmāśeti and Goṇāyi to be the gate through which they came into this world! Blessed again were the people of Pandharpur who could see the Divine playing through these lovers of Viṭṭhala!

The early morning rays of the sun sprinkled gold on the mound of mud. The mist was making way for the sun to spread its warmth. A lonely hut stood amidst the trees and flower bushes. From within the hut, a continual chanting of '*Pāṇḍuraṅga'* in a sweetly gruff voice rang out. It so matched with those sounds of Nature that it appeared to be a part of it. The voice was of another great devotee, Gorā Kumbhār, a potter by profession. He lived in a village of Satyapuri, also known as Ter, not very far from Pandharpur. Connected to Mother Earth as he was, he had all the qualities of Earth – patience, kindness and understanding. In spite of the fact that he was apparently unlettered, his wisdom was truly remarkable. His greatest virtue was his *śraddhā or* total trust in the Existence. For him every being and everything was a manifestation of the Divine. It was not just a thought for him but a reality he lived! He was married to Saṅti, who bore a male child for him.

Though a great devotee of Viṭṭhala, he fulfilled his responsibility of looking after his family by making pots and selling them. However, he would make only so many pots as were needed for the survival of the family! All the time, including that when involved with his trade of pottery, he would be engrossed in chanting the name of Viṭṭhala and Pāṇḍuraṅga.

Knowing the nature of Gorā, Saṅti would keep the baby

with her even when she would go to fetch water. But one day since the child was asleep, she told Gorā to keep an eye on the child as he was sleeping. Gorā, in his trust, said that Pāṇḍuraṅga was keeping an eye on every being and continued to cure the clay under his dancing feet, chanting God's name:

'Meditating on Keśava, the Earth body is dancing on the clay;
Remembering the name of Viṭṭhala time and again,
The water flows from the eyes in gratitude for the good fortune.
In a clan of potters, the body was born,
That Gorā potter, was chosen to be a bhakta *of Hari.'*[45]

The whole area reverberated with the name of Viṭṭhala, and Gorā was lost to the external world. It was as though his body had merged with the sound of his voice, which again spread in entire Existence! In such an ecstatic experience, he started kneading and curing the mud with rivulets of tears flowing down his cheeks, thus wetting the clay! Meanwhile, the child got up from sleep and started crying for its mother. Unable to see her, he started crawling out of the hut and attracted by the resonance of Gorā's chanting, he crawled near to his father. And like his father, who had been calling for the father (Viṭṭhala), he too wanted to capture Gorā's attention. Crying out hoarsely, he went under the father's feet and got crushed to death. Gorā unfortunately, unaware of all that had happened, continued his dance.

When Saṅti returned from the river, she started looking for her child; not finding him inside the hut, she started looking outside. Unable to find him even there, she approached Gorā, who was totally lost to the outside world. But when her eyes fell on the clay that was being cured by Gorā's feet, she was flabbergasted to find that it was full of blood of the mutilated body of the child that was crushed under Gorā's weight. It took

45. केशवाचे ध्यान धरोनी अंतरी। मृत्तीके माझारीं नाचतसे।। १।। विट्ठलाचे नाम स्मरे वेळो वेळा।
नेत्रीं वाहे जळ सद्गती चे।। २।।
कुलालाचे वंशी जन्मले शरीर। तो गोरा कुंभार हरिभक्त।। ३।।

quite some time and her intense shrieks and wails to bring back Gorā to the external reality. His tears of joy changed to those of remorse and sadness. He heard Saṅti shout: "What have you done? The only work I had ever given you was to keep an eye on our child; even that you failed because of your cursed Viṭṭhala whom you are obsessed with. You are mad and cruel. When you are so heartless and indifferent to your own family, how can you possibly claim yourself to be a *bhakta*? God, they say, is very compassionate and kind, how can you be so cruel and callous?"

Gora was silent, unable to say anything to his wife's allegations. She continued amidst unstoppable tears: "I curse you and your Viṭṭhala, who as you say is taking care of the universe. I curse you with the heart of a mother who has lost her only child due to your callousness and irresponsible behaviour, that may you not have anything to do with Viṭṭhala."

Gorā, though sad, did not *react* but responded sadly: "It has been told by the saints, that the love of God demands a lot of sacrifice, and comes at a very high cost. For me, perhaps this had to be the price. My forgetfulness of the world was responsible and I am your culprit. Now I am ready to accept whatever punishment you mete on me." So saying he bent low in salutation.

But as expected, Saṅti could not be consoled by his words. She shouted at him: "I put an *āṇa*, vow, that may you never touch Viṭṭhala again."

Górā bowed low in total acceptance.

Days passed and Gorā stopped touching the idol of Pāṇḍuraṅga or even going near it! But Saṅti noticed that he had also stopped coming near her; even if she offered food, he would ask her to keep the plate near him and take it only when she had gone a distance! He would ask her to keep the vessel of water, lest his fingers touched hers! She asked him one day: "Why is it that you are avoiding me?"

Gorā looked into her eyes and said: "Saṅti, don't you remember your *āṇa* that I should not touch Viṭṭhala again?"

Saṅti protested: "But what I said was that you should not touch the idol of Viṭṭhala and not me, your wife!"

"Saṅti, my dear, Viṭṭhala is in everyone and He is more in you than anyone else! For he is trying to free me of all family activities and *graha saṁsāra*! Moreover, it was not you who gave me this diktat but it was Viṭṭhala who spoke through you! Whatever comes out through anyone's mouth is His. So, I take it as a positive omen for me, that He will show Himself to me."

But involved as she was with her personal tragedy, she played a deaf ear and shouted once again: "Are you mad? What do you think a mother, who has lost her only child, would do? I may have said so many things in anger; do you think I was even capable of thinking straight? Whatever was uttered was in anger. But now I appeal to you, beg of you, to give me a child so that we shall have someone to continue our family. I will not be a woman till I become a mother." There was intense pain in her tone.

Gorā said with all compassion: "Saṅti, let me tell you one great truth, even if you are incapable of understanding what I say: our real family is that of *bhaktas* of Pāṇḍuraṅga, which will continue even without any children of any individual *bhakta*. But yes, I have to be punished for the unforgivable action of mine."

So saying, to the consternation of Saṅti, Gorā cut both his hands. Saṅti wailed at her misfortune: "Now what will we do? At least you used to make a few pots to appease our hunger. What an unfortunate wretch am I?"

Gorā consoled: "Don't be worried; from now on, only Viṭṭhala will look after our needs!"

Saṅti just stared at him in utter dismay! Just then, they heard someone call. On going out, they saw a couple standing at their door. The man asked: "Is this the home of Gorobā Kumbhār?"

Gorā replied: "Yes, it is."

"I am *Sāvaḷā* (dark complexioned) and this is my wife and companion *Sāvḷi* (shadow). We have come from far where there is intense famine. We thought that we would get some work here."

What an irony, thought Gorā, and said: "*Sāvaḷā*, if you had come a little early, I would have been of some help. But now..." he looked at his cut hands.

Sāvaḷā came near him and holding those stunted limbs, said: "Gorobā, only you can help us in this village, because only you have what we need. Just like you, we too are potters. We will be your hands and do all the work, so that both our families can survive, and live happily."

Gorā felt very familiar with this man, who had kind eyes, smiling face and kinder words! Saṅti immediately responded, she had to because who knows her husband may refuse him: "Yes, yes! You can come."

Gorā joined her, "*Sāvaḷā*, this house belongs to Pāṇḍuraṅga, and you are most welcome to stay here!"

Saṅti felt that somewhere her mad husband was right! Where on Earth did this help come from?

□

9
The Minstrel

Govind was happy, very happy when his friend told him that the children who had performed the miracle of making the he-buffalo chant the *Veda* were at Nevāsā. He took the permission of his mother to meet them. *Āyi* had readily agreed on the condition that she would accompany him! He had assured her that he would definitely take her after confirming their location and welfare. Govind started from Paiṭhan immediately and reached Nevāsā on the third day. Like him, many persons were gathered there on hearing about four children who were distributing love for God, in the very place used by Lord Viṣṇu to distribute *amṛta,* elixir to gods and demons! He saw many, mostly from farmer and worker community. Thanks to Jñānadev, he was rid of the touch me not inheritance of Brahmins! He was wonderstruck at the simplicity and ready acceptance of these innocent people. It was evening and he proceeded to the temple where the Quartet stayed.

On seeing him, Muktāyi rushed towards him. She was the same bright, energetic and pure self. She said:

"Govind *Dādā*, where is *Āyi*? Is she keeping good health? How is Vidyādhar *Kākā*?"

Appreciating her enthusiasm and affection, Govind responded:

"Muktāyi, both Āyi and Vidyādhar *Kākā* are well. I thought of seeing you first and then bring *Āyi* next time! In fact, she wanted to come with me, this time itself! Where are Nivṛttidādā, Jñānā and Sopān?" Just then the loud and sweet chanting of '*Jai Jai Rāmakṛṣṇa Hari*' started and he saw the three holy brothers entering the temple. Govind rushed towards them. On seeing him, they were overjoyed and embraced him when he tried to fall prostrate at their feet. There was so much of love oozing out of their eyes that it brought tears to his eyes. He said: "You remember me?!"

Jñānadev said with lot of affection: "How can we ever forget you, Govind? You gave us our *Āyi*!" He looked at Muktāyi who took Govind for refreshments. Govind followed her happily!

'Carrying the task of flags of bhakti
The bold Vaiśṇavas have arrived;
Attendants of Yama, God of death, run away in fear,
As they hear the roar of His name.
The glory of servants of Hari is that,
The Kaḷikāḷa, time of Kali cannot trouble them.
Shouting the name of Viṭṭhala, Viṭhobā,
The bhaktas have found their path to salvation.
These saints, Nivṛtti and Sopān, are great Vaiśṇavas;
And wherever Muktābāi is,
I too am there chanting Nārāyaṇa!
Jñānadev says Vaiśṇavas are great, immersed as they are in the name of Viṭṭhala;
Having taken the great holy bath and the charity (of name);
Always the saints travel the path to Vaikunṭha.'[46]

Jñānadev sang and the whole milieu of the temple got charged with *bhāva*. All their emotions would get channelised towards Viṭṭhala, Govind, Hari, their *Iśṭa*. They had been so

---

46. कुंचे पताकांचे भार। आले वैष्णव डिंगर। भेणें पळती यमकिंकर। नामें अंबर गर्जतसे।। १।।
आले हरिदासांचे थाट। कळिकाळा नाहीं वाट। विट्ठलनामें करिती बोभाट। भक्तां वाट सांपडिली।। २।।
निवृत्ति संत हा सोपान। महावैष्णव कठीन। मुक्ताबाई तेथें आपण। नारायण जपतसे।। ३।।
ज्ञानदेव वैष्णव मोठा। विट्ठलनामे मुक्तपेठा। स्नान दान घडे वैष्णववाटा संत गेले।। ४।।

immersed with this practice that their so-called problems appeared petty! It was not a diversion of the mind from the problems, but focusing of their emotions on to a much greater Ideal. For Govind, who had just arrived at the scene, it was really wonderful. He felt that the innocent and spontaneous singing of *abhaṅgs* with *nāmasmaraṇam* is more effective than the recitation of Vedic *mantras* he had learnt at Paiṭhan. He was sitting next to Sopān who just touched him, and he started flowing with current of emotions he had never felt before.

When everything became silent and peaceful, he heard the sweet voice of Jñānadev: "At my Gurunāth's behest, dear brothers and mothers, I offer you the wisdom that has been our family's boat – a boat that is saving us and has been saving the people of our country from drowning in the *bhavasāgar.* It is the *Śāstra Śrīmad Bhagavad Gītā.* It forms a part of *Mahābhāratam* of Veda Vyāsa *muni* in Sanskrit."

There was a pause in which the audience absorbed what they heard. One farmer got up and asked:

"*Devā*, but we do not know the language of the gods. How will we understand what you say?"

Jñānadev responded sweetly: "*Kākā*, you do not have to know Sanskrit to understand what I will be telling you! 'The words in Marāṭhi will quench your thirst, excelling in taste even the sweetness of nectar; the delicacy of words will make soft melodies of music appear wanting; the charm of fragrance will pale before the phrases. The eloquence so sweet, that the very ears will long for more, while all the senses will rush to grab it. By their very nature, words belong to the sense of hearing; yet the tongue claims the object as hers, in taste. Fragrance is the object of smell, but the fragrance of Marathi words would charm the sense of smell.'[47] We will realise that they are not

---

47. माझा मराठाचि बोलु कौतुके। परि अमृतातेंही पैजांसी जिंके। ऐस अक्षरें रसिकें। मेळवीन।। ६.१४।। जिये कोंवळिकेचेनि पाडें। दिसती नद चे रंग थोडे। वेधें परिमळाचें बीक मोडे। जयाचेनि।। १५।। ऐका रसाळपणाचिया लोभा। का श्रवण चि होति जिभा। बोलें इंद्रियां लागे कळंभा। एकामेकां।। १६।। सहजें शब्दु तरी विषो श्रवणाचा। परि रसना म्हणे हा रसु आमुचा। घ्राणासि भावो जाय परिमळाचा। हा तोचि होईल।। १७।। नवल बोलतीये रेखेची वाहणी। देखतां डोळयांही पुरों लागे धणी। ते म्हणती

speaking of anything new but what you already practice in life. That is, Māṇus *Dharma*, which you are living already, but most probably are not aware! Yes, together we will venture to learn to feel God, everywhere and whenever you want."

Everyone present felt that Jñānadev was talking to them individually, encouraging them to start the pilgrimage of the soul, and was taking their hands into his to lead the way. His eyes appeared to look through them, and was lighting their way into themselves! His voice so captivating, that the minds of the audience had merged into one, to be with him. It was as though Existence was speaking to them, consoling, cajoling and encouraging them through Jñānadev's mouth. Only Nivṛttināth, Sopān and Muktāyi knew that their Jñānā had become a passage to his self, the cosmic self, like a hollow flute to manifest the Divine melody!

"Fights are always over insignificant things: land, power or the objects of senses. But these very things are very important for our survival; how can they be insignificant? They are not so important, because they are *naśwara* – subject to change and death and are temporary. Today you are looking after the land, which a person thinks as his! But is it? The same land was claimed to be theirs by the ancestors of this person! And in near future after his death, it will be claimed by his children and their descendants! Similarly, kingdoms are not really the properties of kings but heirlooms to be transferred safely to the future generations. Moreover, the kings are responsible for the welfare of their citizens. The *Kuru* and *Pāṇḍu* princes, children of two brothers, fought against one another for the ownership of the kingdom. Lord Kṛṣṇa did not leave any stone unturned to bring a compromise between the cousins. But the *Kuru* princes did not listen to the advice and the war became imminent."

Jñānadev then described the way in which the armies of the cousins were getting ready for the battle. He had succeeded in creating a graphic picture and simple and innocent that

---

उगडली खाणीं। रूपाची हे।। १८।।

they were, the audience was totally with him. They could hear the noise of chariots, horses, the kettle drums and war trumpets and soldiers taking their positions. And how in that charged milieu of excitement, anger, concern, fear and such other emotions that we face during war times, Lord Kṛṣṇa brought the chariot drawn by five white caparisoned horses. But when Arjuna beheld the Kuru army, he had a very strong doubt about the very purpose of this war. Was it right to fight just for the sake of a kingdom? He thought that between the two families, theirs was more cultured, so was it not noble for the more cultured to stop this fratricidal war?"

He paused for a while, and then continued: "But what is wrong in feeling bad about killing kith and kin for the sake of the kingdom? You must remember that the Pāṇḍu princes had suffered at the hands of those who were totally unrighteous, cunning, unjust and cruel. And that the war was not initiated by them, but the Kauravas. The Lord encouraging Arjuna and making him understand that it is never right to shun action which is to be performed as duty, forms the subject matter of this great *Śāstra*. After all these years how does it help us, who are not fighting any war? Surviving and living in this *saṁsāra* is also a battle! We face many situations when we get confused about the necessity to get involved in action or to avoid it. The Lord teaches us to differentiate between *dharma* and *adharma*."

Jñānadev pointed out that Arjuna was no ordinary person, a great warrior, a very good human being and a person who had implicit trust in the Lord. It was not at all due to the fear of losing that he was overpowered by this hesitation. His basic doubts were only two: just for the sake of a kingdom why should one indulge in a fratricidal battle, because we enjoy the sovereignty only with our kith and kin. The outcome of this war – that thousands would be killed and families orphaned – was obvious. Another and more important doubt was: are not compassion and love greater virtues to be nurtured and coveted and ambition of winning to be shunned?

Govind had not heard anyone speak in the mother

tongue, which was so sweet and pleasant to the ears. He had memorised all the seven hundred and one verses from *Śrīmad Bhagavad Gītā*, the commentary being in original Sanskrit. He had gone through all the nuances of words and their origin.

But this was something entirely different. Jñānadev was connecting the listeners to the Lord and his devotees and also with one another because they all felt through their hearts! They could identify with Arjuna, his confusion and his problems! Jñānadev was more than right in saying that it is not mandatory to have the knowledge of Sanskrit for acquiring the wisdom of the *Gītā*.

The eastern horizon blushed with happiness as it welcomed the sun – the source of heat and light of the world. It was dawn and the three siblings sat facing Nivṛttināth, their source of spiritual warmth and light! Govind, never far away from them, had joined them, happy to learn and live from what he observed from the Quartet. Though Nivṛttināth was silent, the joy and wisdom that radiated from him could *be felt by him*. Spontaneously, he became part of this team, flowed with them and got drenched in the flood of bliss.

After a while, his mind began its activity and started thinking of the means of being useful to these spiritual siblings of his. Sopān, sitting next to him, just touched his forehead between the brows and he re-entered the internal world!

Slowly, when all of them had their morning feast of bliss and light, Jñānadev looked at Govind and asked: "Govind, it appears that the Lord has chosen you to be the scribe for His *satsaṅga*."

It was as though Jñānadev had responded to the query he had during the *sādhanā*. He responded: "Jñānadev, the Lord has heard my prayers, I shall do your bidding. Blessed am I to be of some service."

Jñānadev smiled and said: "Govind, the Lord wanted us to meet so that we could all be His instruments in completing His work."

That afternoon, a group of persons came from Paiṭhan

to Nevāsa. Among them were Vidyādhar Śāstri and a few others who had been spiritually attracted to the Quartet. Most important among them was Bhāmātāī, mother of Govind. Muktāyi ran to her and hugged her as intensely as a child to her mother! The brothers came and prostrated. While her eyes were only on these divine siblings, she saw Govind only when he came running to her. He asked: "*Āyi*, how did you come?"

Caressing his cheek, she said: "I knew that once you came to these children of mine, you will not even think of me, let alone come to fetch me! When I came to know of Vidyādhar *Bhāvu*[48] making a pilgrimage to Nevāsā, I joined them! Your face reflects the treasure you are acquiring during these days!" Whatever she had said was true and Govind thought it better to be silent than explain and so he smiled. Govind was with his mother, without any effort of going back to Paiṭhan for bringing her to Nevāsā. 'God is great,' he thought. Was it then the same principle that had chosen him to be the medium to become a scribe for Jñānadev or this divine Quartet that was responsible? He cared less, but was extremely happy at the ways things were turning out for him and his mother.

Bhāmātāī and Muktāyi had much to share, including the responsibility of the common kitchen which fed those who came for *satsaṅga* from other places and who chose to stay back at Nevāsā. This group was steadily swelling day by day, for the news was spreading fast that Jñānadev was giving inspired discourses on the essence of *Śrīmad Bhagavad Gītā* in Marāṭhi, and that it was not only relevant to all persons including the common man, but was totally simple and comprehensible! And that the atmosphere he created was ethereal and divine and should not be missed.

> *'The golden day has dawned, as there is a downpour of Nectar.*
> *We saw Hari and are seeing Hari, who has enveloped us from within and without.*
> *On the stable brick of steady mind, He stands adorned with*

48. Brother in Marathi.

garland of wild flowers.
In this great gathering of saints, manifests the self-satisfied!
Ocean of compassion the ever graceful Father, the companion of Rakhumādevi.'[49]

There was celebration in the temple with the devotees singing and enjoying the blissful voice of Jñānadev. The groups of persons from Paiṭhan, especially Vidyādhar, were immersed in the ocean of emotions and their own tears! The farmers and the craftsmen were ecstatic and dancing. They had one more *abhaṅg* in their stock. It had become their normal routine to sing the *abhaṅg* heard in the evening before, when they worked in their respective fields or trades. Bhāmātāī was beside with tears of joy, to flow with the *bhāvas* created by the *abhaṅg*! At the same time, a small thorn of regret was pricking her, 'What if Rukmiṇi was with her just now?' She felt a soft touch on her back, and when she looked for its origin, she found Muktāyi smiling. She returned to the ongoing feast of nectar with a thought: 'instead of one, now I have five children. Is it not *kṛpā*, grace of God?'

As the strains of *'Jai Jai Rāmakṛṣṇa Hari'* slowly got merged into silence, the nectar-like voice of Jñānadev rose, pleasing the ears of one and all:

"At the command of my Gurunāth, I ventured into this difficult task of offering you the essence of the *Bhagavad Gītā* in our mother tongue. But first we need to answer the question: Really is there any need? In fact, it is the need of the hour. This *Śāstra* was meant to be known by everyone in the society; not only to be known, but to be lived. During *Dwāpara yuga*[50] when *Mahābhāratam* was written, Sanskrit

49. आजि सोनियाचा दिनु। वर्षे अमृताचा घनु।। १।। हरि पाहिला रे हरि पाहिला रे।
सबाह्याभ्यंतरि अवघा व्यापक मुरारी।। २।।
दृढ विटे मन मुळी। विराजित वनमाळी।। ३।। बरवा संतसमागमु। प्रगटला आत्मारामु।। ४।।
कृपासिंधु करुणाकरू। बापरखुमादेवि-वरू।। ५।।

50. Our culture divides time into four *yugas* of *Satya, Treta, Dwāpara and Kali.* The cow of *dharma* stands on all four legs in *Satya yuga*; three legs in *Treta yuga*; two in *Dwāpara yuga*; and on one in *Kali yuga.*

was the language of the common people. But over the ages, and especially now, it has become the language of the scholars. Time is ripe for all to reclaim it from the forests of complicated words and their interpretations. How could it be otherwise? Lord Kṛṣṇa took the help of Arjuna to freely distribute it to all and sundry. In this divided society of the high and the low, of the sacred and the profane, we need to know that *paramātman* has no boundaries and borders; all is one without the second. As He resides in every one of us, He is everything. It gives out the common code of conduct to every member of the society. It was Ādi Śaṅkarācārya who brought this portion out of *Mahābhāratam* and declared it as a *Śāstra*."

Jñānadev remembered the contribution made by this great visionary. His all-inclusive attitude and his all-encompassing love for existence. Jñānadev also felt sad as the commentaries written by the prodigy were reduced to hair-splitting arguments and became the exclusive rights of *Pundits*! Hopefully, this venture he had taken up at the insistence of his *guru*, Nivṛttināth would free the scripture from the holds of the pedantry and bring it to the common mass of people who are simple, pure, unassuming and loving. And he was confident that the need of the society alone had made him and his siblings instrumental in accepting this responsibility. He remembered his dear father, who had given this scripture as a parting gift. Wiping tears from the eyes he resumed: "Lord Kṛṣṇa commenced his discourse, with an admonition to Arjuna as to how a brave and wise man like him could ever entertain cowardice and ignorance in his mind. With an intention of dissolving ignorance from Arjuna totally, He started treating the problem in all the dimensions of life. First of all, *Bhagavān* said that one should have an understanding that all experiences we have through the contact of senses with their respective objects giving rise to the perceptions like heat and cold or happiness and misery, are fleeting and temporary. That is why, we should endure them.[51] This *Śloka*

51. मात्रास्पर्शास्तु कौन्तेय शीतोष्णसुखदुःखदाः। आगमापायिनोऽनित्यास्तांस्तितिक्षस्व भारत।। २.१४।।

gives us the *manasthiti, the* mental attitude to face life and all its trials and tribulations."

Jñānadev gratefully remembered his dear father's advice and how it had helped all of them to take life boldly. He continued: "This world and Nature that we see, which envelops everything, is temporary. The state of body keeps changing from infanthood, to childhood, to youth, middle age, and old age. At the same time, who experiences these changes and also remembers them? One sees the sunrise and experiences its beauty. In a short time, the atmosphere changes and it is so with all our experiences. When we realise this through our own experience, the mind loses its rigidity. When it does, one also learns something more important: there is this memory of the experience and maybe he or she tries to re-live it! The world outside has changed but there is someone who does not change, who remembers. The search for this entity, which is beyond any change, which experiences and remembers is the beginning of the pilgrimage of *adhyātma*, spirituality. Why should we seek that which is eternal? Because we want to get rid of our misery, which is there in the duality of *sukha-dukha*, happiness-misery, in the impermanent, in the evanescent. Every one of us knowingly or unknowingly is on this grand pilgrimage. The details of this search are given by the Lord in this scripture."

Vidyādhar Shastri, who sat just in front of Nivṛttināth, was overpowered by a host of emotions, like guilt, regret and sadness on one side and joy, blessedness and celebration on the other! He had met Viṭṭhalpant and had genuine appreciation for his wonderful understanding on spirituality, but Vidyādhar had been carried away by the opinion of the society! He realised that it was basically the fear that had made many like him fanatical at Āḷandi. When these thoughts were going on in his mind, Vidyādhar's eyes met with those of Nivṛttināth, bringing an end to the train of thoughts and replacing it with calmness and composure!

Jñānadev's bell-like voice overwhelmed him: "Action is

the principal facet of life. Life without action is equivalent to death. To survive, we need to put effort. So, the Lord gave the secret of action through which *karma*, action, ordinary or special, can get transformed to *karma yoga*. Just as we do not have any choice in our birth, which comes to us based on our past actions, we do not have any choice in the work. O mothers and brothers, let me assure you that work is neither sacred nor profane, nor high nor low. How we perform the action that has come to our lot makes it so! If you perform the action with complaint, jealousy, anger and similar negative feelings, it becomes profane and low. If you perform it as your duty unselfishly in joy as though it has been given by Rāmakṛṣṇa, Hari, Viṭṭhala, and do it for *Him*, the action becomes a *pūjā*.[52] How can we turn our so-called ordinary work, any work, into worship? By remembering the Lord, who has allotted the work to us! Let us take His name, *Jai Jai Rāmakṛṣṇa Hari*!"

With that everyone in the assembly joined the chorus and was happy and felt blessed to be in this *satsaṅga* which was giving them so much joy and more importantly, was transforming them!

> '*He is everywhere, in everybody; but man is unaware of Him.*
> *Supreme is bitter while sense-object sweet; that is why there is conflict in* saṁsāra.
> *Fix the arrow of* nāma, *name, to the bow of tongue; for such a one He is very near.*
> *If there is constant grit and courage; such a one has heaven of love in heart.*
> *Jñānadev knows that the wise ones are aware of this principle;*
> Nāma *alone is the panacea for all conflict and sins.*'[53]

---

52. Swami Vivekananda gave a prompt '*Work is Worship*' for developing this attitude.

53. सर्व व्यापक सर्व देह आहे। परि प्राणियांसि सोये न कळे तयाची।। परमार्थ तो कडू विषय तो गोडु। तया अवघडु संसारू।।
नामाचे साधन जिह्वे लावी बाण। तया अनुदिन जवळ वसे।। धारणा धीट ज़रि होये विनट।

Jñānadev sang, beheld all those gathered in the temple affectionately and with attention. Some noted with pleasant surprise that his look was directed not only towards those attending the *satsaṅga* but towards the whole universe, for he had accommodated it in his being! Soon as the *abhaṅg* concluded, they all joined in the chorus of *Jai Jai Rāmakṛṣṇa Hari*. When Nivṛttināth looked at the ecstatic crowd, he noted with satisfaction that many of them, especially the simple farmers and tradesmen, had succeeded in using their tongues as bows and *nāma* as arrows effectively! He closed his eyes in veneration of his parents and *guru*, Gahinināth.

After the chorus and minds of the audience had settled down in silence, Jñānadev started speaking: "The essence of *Śrīmad Bhagavad Gītā* is understood and lived by those who have acquired *Arjuna-bhāva*, the mood of Arjuna. What is *Arjuna-bhāva*? From the very first meeting, he had become a *sakhā*, friend of the Lord and that happens to be the eighth method of *bhakti* known as *sakhya*. Over the years, Arjuna had total trust in the Lord and had totally surrendered to Him, and thus had stepped into *ātmanivedana*, the ninth method of *bhakti.* Before going to Hastināpura for a peace truce with the Kauravas, the Lord had asked each of the Pāṇḍavas their wish. Yudiṣṭira and Nakula had asked for peace; Sahadeva had predicted that there could be no truce and hence war was inevitable; Bhīma and Draupadi wanted war; they even told the Lord not even to try! When Lord Kṛṣṇa approached Arjuna, he said he was sure that whatever the Lord's wish will be in favour of the Pāṇḍavas! During the preparations for the war, Duryodhana and Arjuna approached the Lord for help. They found the Lord fast asleep. Duryodhana, unwilling to stand near the feet, chose to sit near the head, while Arjuna, who came later, happily stood near the feet, enjoying the ethereal face of the Lord! When the Lord got up, he saw Arjuna first and asked him his wish. Arjuna, gestured to Lord that Duryodhana

---

तया प्रेम वैकुंठ जवळ असे।।

ज्ञानियासि ज्ञान ज्ञानदेव ध्यान। कलि मल च्छेदन नाम एक।।

had come before him and so he should be asked first. Lord smiled and said that since He had seen Arjuna first he should be the first to choose! The Lord placed the choice before the two cousins: on one side his entire army, and on the other, He would be but without any weapons!

"Arjuna chose the Lord, while Duryodhana was very happy to get the well-equipped Yādava army! When Duryodhana left, the Lord asked Arjuna as to why he had chosen wrongly, in spite of getting the first choice. Arjuna had said that he did not need any army to defeat the Kauravas, but he wanted the Lord on his side. Such was the relationship between Arjuna and the Lord. No wonder Lord Kṛṣṇa chose Arjuna for preaching the *Gītā*. Dear brothers, sisters and mothers, let us try to get into the *bhāva* of Arjuna. Most of you are not only simple, but have trust in your heart. But some of you who have the weight of high birth and education in your being, must try to shake the load off your hearts. Pride and egotism are really unnecessary burdens to carry on our pilgrimage towards God realisation."

The audience, especially those who had come from Paiṭhan and some from Āḷandi, became conscious, but Jñānadev's compassionate look put them at ease!

> *'Does the seed come out of fruit or is it the seed that begets the fruit?*
> *No one can understand them O God!*
> *Is the Earth made of clay or the clay the product of Earth?*
> *Such questions on the cause and effect cannot be known.*
> *Only experience becomes the witness to their dissolution!*
> *O Father, companion of Rakhumādevi, You dwell within and envelop without.'*[54]

Jñānadev took his audience to a different dimension, beyond intellectual jugglery and argument; beyond the habit of looking down on others, by demonstrating that every being is special if he is on a pilgrimage of seeking the eternal within

54. फळाच बीज बीजाच फळ। म्हणूनि पत्र पुष्प मूळ चोजवे ना।। ऐसी हे रचना न कळे ग देवा। सिद्धान्त अनुभवा साक्ष देतो।। मृत्तिकेची पृथ्वी की पृथ्वीची मृत्तिका। ही गति अनेका चोजवे ना।। बाप रखुमादेवी वरु निरंतरी। सबाह्य अभ्यंतरी नांदतसे।।

the temporal. The only thing required for this pilgrimage is the righteous conduct, which too is effortless if one develops the *bhāva*, that there is no difference whatsoever between the creation and the Creator, because Creator has become the creation!

He began his discourse: "The Lord declares in the *Bhagavad Gītā* that for feeling Him, for being with Him, whenever you are involved in any action, you have the attitude that 'He is all aspects of action as well as the one who acts.'[55] Gradually, when this attitude matures into a conviction, you start realising that actually, you are not the performer of any action, but a non-involved witness.[56] See the compassion of the Lord! If this is not possible, then learn *ātma-saṁyama*, self-control."

Thereafter, Jñānadev went on to describe the nuances of yoga, as practised by the Nāth tradition, in detail. As it had been the experience, he had gained under the tutelage of Nivṛttināth, he went into raptures! Though *Gītā* makes only passing remarks, Jñānadev had brought out the secret of yoga for the common mass of people in their own language!

Having heard of the ongoing spontaneous discourses on the *Gītā* in simple Marathi by Jñānadev at Nevāsa, unable to restrain his affection for the Quartet and the thirst to learn, Gangādhar Shastri had left Āḷandi to reach Nevāsā. When he listened in rapt attention, he felt happy that he had tried his best to get them a respectable place in the society of Āḷandi. Though he had failed, he now felt blessed that he had decided to leave the *dharma-sabhā* and take shelter under the *Kalpavṛkṣa*, the wish-fulfilling tree of real spirituality! He experienced the joy and ecstasy of the people, mostly simple and innocent.

---

55. ब्रह्मार्पणं ब्रह्म हविब्रह्माग्नौ ब्रह्मणा हुतम्। ब्रह्मैव तेन गन्तव्यं ब्रह्मकर्मसमाधिना।।
श्रीम्भगवद्गीता ४.२४।।

56. नैव किन्चित्करोमीति युक्तो मन्येव तत्ववित्।
पश्यन्शृण्वन्स्पृशन्जिघ्रत्रश्नन्गच्छन्स्वपन्श्वसन्।। ५.८।।
प्रलपन्विसृजन्गृह्णत्रुन्मिषत्रिमिषत्रपि। इन्द्रियाणीन्द्रियार्थेषु वर्तन्त इति धारयन्।। श्रीम्भगवद्गीता ५.९।।

It was his first day at Nevāsā when he noticed a middle-aged man shedding tears, while listening to Jñānadev. After the discourse, he approached him and asked: "*Kākā*, I saw you shedding tears throughout the discourse. Is something troubling you?"

How was he to know that this man was Dhoṅḍu, the farmer who harvested love?! Dhoṅḍu laughed and responded: "Nothing troubles me anymore! For I am under the shelter of *Deva* (Jñānadev)! All my so-called problems have dissolved!"

Still wondering, Gangādhar asked: "Then, why were there the unstoppable tears in your eyes, *Kākā*?"

Dhoṅḍu smiled and looked at the seat on which Jñānadev sat while discoursing, with a distant look, said: "When he spoke today, I did not understand a word he said. But wonder of wonders, throughout the discourse I saw the Lord Himself, speaking to Arjuna. Seeing this wondrous sight, my heart swelled up and tears of bliss started flowing on their own. How could I and why I should I stop them?"

Gangādhar spontaneously fell at the feet of this simple and yet a great man, who just lifted him to take him in warm embrace. It was Gangādhar's turn to shed the tears of bliss! When he regained his composure, Gangādhar approached the mart of joy consisting of the Quartet – Govind, Vidyādhar and others. Vidyādhar rushed to welcome him. Nivṛttināth, Jñānadev, Sopāndev and Muktāyi welcomed him.

Muktāyi rushed and touched his feet while Gangādhar reacted: "No Muktāyi, it is I, who should prostrate before you all!"

Jñānadev responded: "Gangādhar *Kākā* you are elder to us." They all fell at his feet.

When he saw Dhoṅḍu standing and enjoying the scene, he said: "Dhoṅḍu *Kākā*, he has come from Āḷandi. Gangādhar *Kākā*, it was Dhoṅḍu *Kākā* who opened my heart!"

Gangādhar said with the same respect: "Jñānadev, Dhoṅḍu *Kākā* has performed the miracle on me too! My heart too has opened."

Some farmers were taking the three brothers and a group of devotees around the town of Nevāsā. When they reached *amritavāhini* they saw a crowd of people, who had been waiting for them, singing *Jai Jai Rāmakṛṣṇa Hari* in perfect rhythm and tune. Jñānadev gestured to his companions to silently join them without disturbing the ongoing rhythm. When the farmers stopped their *nāmasmaraṇam*, they welcomed them. Jñānadev looked at his companions.

Govind asked: "Jñānadev, you are deliberate in performing every action. Why was it that you asked us not to disturb? They would have never got disturbed?"

Jñānadev paused and responded: "Govind, the gesture was not for them, but for us! They chose to take the name of the Lord and were lost to the world. When we approached them, we were very much in and of the world! To get into the dimension of the Lord, we have to be silent within as well as without. Moreover, even in this beautiful dimension of the Lord we call the world, we don't really need the noise of name and fame, or of fight and dissension! We can enter the world silently, and silently can we leave as guests in someone else's house."

How true, felt all of them! Most of all Gangādhar and Vidyādhar, who had spent most of their life in hair-splitting discussions and arguments about *dharma* and *adhyātma*, without ever considering to practice them! In the meantime, the farmers welcomed them and offered them refreshments.

> 'Yogis *seek the vision of the Beloved by renouncing the world;*
> *And they never succeed in seeing Him;*
> *They get lost in the mire of arguments and descriptions instead.*
> *I saw and am seeing the Lord of gods;*
> *The doubt of otherness got dissolved.*
> *Saw You in infinite costumes and infinite forms.*
> *In spite of all this, wonder of wonders, my taste for*

Father Viṭṭhala, companion of Rakhumādevi never receded!'[57]

The whole milieu was vibrant with the mood of Jñānadev. Everyone without exception could feel that the minstrel in Jñānadev was living the spirit of the *abhaṅg*! Today it was something different, something or someone unknown and perhaps unknowable had descended into this temple. When they heard the sweet voice of Jñānadev, they were all ears:

"Though we spoke of many dimensions of our life and the different approaches to the Divine through action (*Karma yoga*), will (*Dhyāna yoga*), intellect (*Buddhi yoga*), I would like to offer you today and perhaps for this age of Kali, a path that is easy without any arrogance of effort, life affirmative without the pride of renunciation, and blissful in spite of the thorn of the daily vicissitudes of the world!"

He paused so that everyone in the assembly was with him. His voice gathered all of them to envelope in his universal love, Jñānadev spoke: "It is the path of love, of acceptance, and of total surrender: *Bhakti*! My dear self in all of you, the beauty is that while remembering the dialogue of the Lord with Arjuna, we walked this path! Keeping the world aside, negating the attention on it, when we achieve the quietness of the mind, it is called as *dhyāna*. But seeing the Lord with and in the world is *abhidhyāna*!" At this insight, the whole assembly was deluged by a strange intimacy and full silence. Then they heard his voice again:

"The experience of oneness, without the other, which we experience now, is more real than the one we usually deal. Let me whisper one more great Truth, the *ātman*, is our Māvuli, who is more eager to take all of us in her bosom."

It had been nearly three years since the Quartet had started staying at Nevāsa for spreading the essence of *Śrīmad Bhagavad Gītā*. Scholars, who had tasted the sweetness of

57. योगियां दुर्लभ तो म्यां देखिला साजणी। पाहतां पाहतां मना न पुरे धणी।।
देखिला देखिला माये देवांचा देवो। फिटला संदेहो निमाले दूजेपण।।
अनंत वेष अनंत रुपे देखिला तयासि। बाप रखुमादेवी-वरु खूण बाणली कैसी।।

Bhāvārthadīpikā, the interpretation of the *Śāstra* by Jñānadev, were more than convinced that the *Gītā* was not merely a translation into the sweet language of Marathi but was a trans-creation! The swelling audience had transcended the boundaries of caste, gender and status. This had been possible by *bhakti*, which takes us beyond the discrimination through mutual respect and love, compassion and help.

Jñānadev insisted on seeing and experiencing the Divine in everything and everywhere. Instead of stressing on the fact that the Divine is *nirākāra* – formless and *nirguṇa* – without any quality, he insisted that the Divine has infinite forms and qualities! He declared that this attitude helps the *bhakta* to be with the Divine and in the Divine all the time! It was time for the Quartet to meet other seekers treading the path.

□

10
The Gathering

Persons having a soft corner for orphaned children of Vitthalpant and Rukminidevi, some of whom had also the feeling of guilt, had reached Nevāsā from Alandi. They were awestruck to note that the four children, who had suffered and suffered intensely, were extremely happy to receive them. Some of them even felt that perhaps the Quartet had forgotten that phase of life! In a way they were right because the collective mind of the Quartet had become as pure as the crystal-clear water on which whatever is written can never remain; it disappears soon as the finger is removed from its surface! But how could they possibly know that these so-called orphaned children had found their real parents in *Ātma* Māvuli? But they all agreed on one point – that the rightful place for Nivrttinath, Jñānadev, Sopāndev and Muktāyi was Āḷandi, which had the privilege of being their birthplace. When they approached the Quartet with the proposal, nay appeal, it was readily agreed. Nivrttinath however, had one request to the people and that was – they would stay in the same hut in which they were born! Some of them rushed to Āḷandi to carry the glad tidings of the arrival of the Quartet to Āḷandi.

On their journey back to Āḷandi, Nivṛttināth, Jñānadev, Sopāndev, Muktāyi and others reached a small village named Puṇatambe, where a great *yogi*, Cāngadev by name, had his *āśrama*. It was believed that his age was fourteen hundred years and during his long and arduous penance, he had acquired *yogic siddhis*, powers. Wanting to meet him and pay their respects, they reached the place of the great *yogi's* place of penance, and found him in deep *samādhi*. A small group of hopeful people was waiting for the *yogi* to come out of his *samādhi*. Compassionate that Muktāyi was, she went near them to enquire the reason for their sadness. She noticed a dead body of a teenaged boy. His father and relatives had brought the body with the fond hope of Cāngadev reviving the boy back to life. They had been waiting for hours. She just went near the body and caressed the forehead of the boy. Miraculously, he sat up to the joyful surprise of his relatives.

Finding no sign of the *yogi* returning to worldly consciousness, and as their onward journey was being delayed, Nivṛttināth and his group continued their journey to Āḷandi. The group of pilgrims sat in a place with a small meandering stream, under an old banyan to relax. They still had one more day to walk to reach Āḷandi. Though the Quartet had already forgotten the Puṇatambe incident, it was very much in the mind of Govind, who wanted to talk about it but was hesitant. Nivṛttināth being aware of Govind's mind addressed him: "Govind, something seems to disturb you. What is it?"

Govind said self-consciously: "Mahārāj, we have been listening to saints and also reading about them. They say that we should never disturb the laws of Nature. The boy had died because it was time for him to depart. Don't you think that Muktāyi's action of reviving him was against Nature?"

Nivṛttināth laughed loudly and asked Govind instead: "How do you know that his time of departure had come?" He paused and then continued: "Govind, remember, Existence is *anaṅta*, endless as well as *śāsvata*, eternal and we are nothing compared to it! So, whatever happens in it is preordained and all of us are but its instruments through which He acts! He had something to achieve through the action of Muktāyi."

Nivṛttināth looked at Jñānadev, who saluted him before speaking: "Gurudev, the mood of Muktāyi that propelled her is also extremely important. Looking at the intense suffering of the relatives on the boy's death made her feel the pain with the same intensity. She felt one with the group. Such empathy and sympathy expand the heart so much that it merges with the will of Existence. When she caressed the forehead of the boy, it was really not Muktāyi, but Śri Viṭṭhala acting through her! The expansion appears to be the sole secret of *bhakti, universal love*, when the individual ego dissolves into the cosmic will."

When they reached Āḷandi, there was a grand reception with the mothers and sisters welcoming their children with joyous tears and open arms. Almost every person was curious to meet the siblings, who had bounced back in spite of unjust persecution meted out to them and who, instead of grouse against their persecutors, had only understanding, compassion and love for them. They saw clearly that the Quartet would help anyone and everyone who came to them. Almost all of them experienced a joy never felt before; a strange feeling of intimacy, with not only the Quartet, but the whole of Āḷandi, never experienced before. They wanted to be a part of the renaissance of the revival of spirituality.

Gangādhar Śāstri noted that Visobā Pant was missing. When enquired, he was told that he was angrier on the Quartet for hypnotising the innocent people of Āḷandi and that the destruction of Āḷandi was now imminent! Gangādhar felt that Visobā was now eligible only for pity because he was refusing to face the light by holding on to darkness, and suffering by nurturing negative emotions, instead of participating in the celebration of purity, growth and bliss. The subject of Gangādhar's musings was really suffering. His wife and dear daughter Namu had openly disobeyed him and joined the welcome function given by the town.

Sītābāī had gathered her friends and their daughters for cleaning and decorating the hut, once occupied by Viṭṭhalpant and Rukmiṇidevi, and their children. During this time, she had wiped her tears time and again, remembering how her dear friend would have been ecstatic. But the purity of the fortunate couple, who were the gate through which these divine children entered the world, had been vindicated.

At Puṇatambe, in the *āśrama* of Yogi Cāngadev, the situation was different. When the great *yogi* came out of his *samādhi*, the disciples narrated the whole incident in which a young girl had revived a dead boy by just touching the forehead; and that the four divine children had waited for their *guru* for quite some time, but not finding any signs of his coming down to worldly dimension (!), they had left for Āḷandi. The *yogi* noted wonder and appreciation in the narration of his disciples and was piqued.

However, curiosity got better of the *yogi* and so he made more enquiries about the children. He then recalled the plight of Viṭṭhalpant who was excommunicated for *falling from sanyāsa* to *gṛhastāśrama*. Wanting to meet these children, he began writing a letter to invite all of them to his *aśrama*. There however, was the problem of addressing Jñānadev?! How should he address Jñānadev in the salutation of the letter?

Jñānadev was just fifteen-years old, while he was of fourteen hundred years; Jñānadev was just beginning his journey while he had matured like the banyan under which he sat; and yet, from what he had heard, these four children were so wonderful that in spite of all the persecution by the society, they had no complaint against anyone. Instead, they had unbounded love for whoever they met! He kept thinking for quite a while only to finally decide to send a blank letter! He told his disciples that if he understood the contents of the blank letter, Jñānadev would definitely send a suitable reply or else it was not worth meeting him!

The messengers of Cāngadev reached the abode of the Quartet at Āḷandi. It was noon and the three brothers were in their *madhyānnikā*, the noon worship. Muktāyi received them, requesting them to wait till her brothers finished their worship and proceeded to make arrangements for the meal. The disciples were surprised at the humility and unconditional love for them by this child wonder, who had revived a dead boy! Soon the brothers emerged out of the hut to meet the disciples of Yogi Cāngadev who handed over the letter of their *guru*. On opening the letter, Nivṛttināth smiled who handed it to Jñānadev, who too smiled.

Muktāyi, who was nearby, took the letter and laughed loudly on looking at the blank letter! She commented: "So Nivṛtti *Dādā*, *Mahāyogi* Cāngadev is still blank in spite of so many years of *tapas*!"

Jñānadev said quite seriously: "No Muktāyi, one should not make fun of someone's *tapas*; we should respect it. Cāngadev just has some doubts and wants us to clarify. Please offer food to his disciples; they must be tired and hungry after their journey on foot from Puṇatambe."

He looked at Govind and started reciting: "Śrīvaṭeśu[58], be blessed! The Supreme Spirit by hiding itself creates the appearance of the world. Then by absorbing it into itself, reveals itself...Just as the gold gets transformed into ornaments without losing its quality, the Supreme self becomes the world without any loss...Sārī is only a name of the thread; the earthen pot is only clay...All the ornaments though called by various names are gold in totality, or as the various limbs of the body, though mistaken to be separate, belong to one body. All the elements, right from Śiva to Earth which appear as different substances, shine alike with the same pure consciousness. Paintings depict all sorts of pictures but behind them is a wall alone on which the pictures are drawn. So, the pure consciousness shines in the form of universe...Without getting tainted by happiness or sorrow, He spontaneously bestirs himself and assumes various forms of objects to appear before Himself... That way, the supreme spirit goes on showing itself in the

58. Cāngadev's title.

form of various objects created out of self to only self, thereby appearing as the Tripuṭi of seer, seeing and seen...In this way, the pure consciousness appears threefold. Know this well-known principle of the creation of the universe...The supreme spirit cannot be expressed; it cannot be comprehended by any means; you see that It is. The eyes which can see are incapable of seeing themselves; the one who is knowledge incarnate is unable to know his own self!...O Cāngayā! You are the son of that Vaṭeśwara (*guru* of Cāngadev) like pure camphor. So be aware of It (the supreme spirit), the topic of our discussion.

"Jñānadev says, listening to, is like the palm of a hand clasping itself. As speech listening speech, taste tasting the taste or the illuminator seeing light, our conversation is like gold having the coating of gold or face becoming a mirror for the face, O Cakrapāṇi (another name of Cāngadev). Our mutual affection is like the sweetness tasting its own sweetness, contained in the mouth. O my bosom friend, I thirst to meet you; however, I am afraid that the already accomplished meeting may get disturbed...Now transcending the adjectives of 'I and you' the meeting alone is enjoyed over and again, by narrating it...O Cāngayā! More and more treasure of wisdom will come to your door and you will occupy the seat which is beyond the knower and knowledge. O Cāngadevā! Making you as an excuse, the motherly Śrī Nivṛttināth, out of affection for you, has made me offer this sweet-dish of experience... Jñānadev says that it is like the interweaving of sleeping state which transcends the ordinary sleep and the waking state which swallows the natural waking state."[59]

---

59. स्वस्ति श्रीवटेशु। जो लपोनि जगदाभासु। दावी मग ग्रासु। प्रगटला करी।। १।। सान सोनेपणा उण। न येतांचि झाल लेण। त वि न वेचतां जग होण। अंग जया।। ४।। जेवि नाममात्र लुगड। येर्हव सूताचि त उघड। कां माती मृद्भांड। जयापरी।। ९।। अलंकार येण नाम। असिजे निखिल हेम। नाना अवयवसंभ्रम। अवयवियां जेव।। ११।। तेवि शिवोनि पृथ्वीवरी। भासती पदार्थचिया परी। प्रकाश ते एकसरी। संवित्ति हे।। १२।। नाह त चित्र दाविती। परि असे केवळ भिंती। प्रकाश त संवित्ति। जगदाकार।। १३।। न लपतां सुख दुख। येण आकार क्षोभोनि नावेक। होय आपणिया सन्मुख। आपणाचि जो।। १६।। तैस न वचतां भेदा। संवित्ति गमे त्रिधा। हकृचि जाणे प्रसिद्धा। उपपत्ति हिया।। २१।। जे म्हणतां नये कांह। जाणो नये कैसेही। असतचि असे पाही। असणे जया।। ३०।। तया पुत्र तूं वटेश्वराचा। रवा जैसा

So responded Jñānadev to the blank letter of Cāngadev, in sixty-five *ovi-s*, verses! This came to be known as *Cāngadev pāsaṣṭi* – sixty-five verses for Cāngadev. Jñānadev had finished reciting even before Cāngadev's disciples returned! They were pleasantly surprised, as they had seen their master struggling to even start his letter. When they left Āḷandi, they had deep love and regards for the Quartet. Sopāndev, as was his wont, sat silently near Jñānadev, observing this event that he knew would have a lasting impression. When he looked with wonder and respect at this dear elder brother of his, a doubt crept in his consciousness. Even before he expressed it, Jñānadev said with an ethereal smile: "Sopān, you are wondering whether such a long reply was necessary for the blank letter. In spite of his long and arduous effort, Yogi Cāngadev is yet to see the light. Sadly, he got entangled with the *siddhis*, the supernatural powers, which one acquires on way! This letter will increase his thirst in the desirable dimension. He may be able to understand the words of the letter, but his thirst to know the spirit of these words will make him seek. His association will definitely help us and the work that has been entrusted to us. It is a great blessing that Mahāyogi Cāngadev was given such a long life for our sake. In this manifestation and also our experience of God, there is no stranger because every being is connected intimately with all others. Remember Sopān, friend, foe, relation, stranger and their natures, like kind-cruel, good-bad are all but *upādhi-s*, adjectives."

There was absolutely no pride of knowledge in his tone. His intention was clearly to help Cāngadev, a fellow seeker, out

---

कापुराचा। चांगया मज तुज आपणयाचा। बोल ऐके।। ३७।। ज्ञानदेवा म्हणे। तुज माझा बोल ऐकण। त तळहातां तळ मिठी देण। जयापरी।। ३८।। बोल चि बोल ऐकिजे। स्वाद चि स्वाद चाखिजे। कां उजिवड देखिजे। उजिडा जे व।। ३९।। सोनियां वरकल सोन जोसा। कां मुख मखां हो आरिसा । मज तुज संवाद तोसा। चक्रपाणि।। ४०।। गोडिसे आपली गोडी। घेतां काय न माये ता ड। आम्हां पास्पर आवडी। तो पाडु असे।। ४१।। सखया तुझेनि उद्देश। भेटवया जीव उल्हासे। क सिद्धभेटी विसकुसे। ऐसिया बिहे।। ४२।। आतां मा तूं उपाधि। ग्रासुनी भेटी नुसुधी। ते भेगिली अनुवाद। घोळघोळूं।। ५३।। चांगया पुढतपुढती। घरां आलिया ज्ञानसंपत्ति। वेद्यवेदकत्वहि अतीत। पद बैसे।। ६०।। चांगदेवा तुझेनि व्याज। माउलिया श्रीनिवृत्तिराज। स्वानुभव रसाळ खाज। दिधल लोभ।। ६१।। निदेपरैतकृ निदैजण। जागृति गिळोनि जागण। केल तैस गुंफण। ज्ञानदेवो म्हणे।। ६५।।

of pure love for him and his involvement in the work ahead.

Having received the reply, Cāngadev was clearly disturbed. It took him quite a while to understand the spirit behind the letter. He saw no malice or pride, but only affection and surprisingly, intimacy. They had not met, but it appeared as though he had known Jñānadev for ages. On the other hand, he felt a pang of jealousy at the news that Jñānadev's sister, a mere child, had revived the dead boy. Moreover, he discovered that his disciples were changed persons after returning from Āḷandi! And so, he decided to visit Āḷandi to have an audience with them. But since humility was not one of his virtues, he wanted to make his meeting grand and dramatic!

At Āḷandi almost everyone was happy that the children of banished Viṭṭhalpant and Rukmiṇi had been accepted and they felt that their sin of persecution of these innocent children had been absolved. Visobā was an exception as he looked down upon the members of *dharma sabhā* for being so faint hearted as to divert from the path of righteousness and real *dharma*! But even this looking down was a mask to hide his disappointment over the failure to convince his friends! When he heard of Cāngadev's visit to Āḷandi to meet the Quartet, he rushed to Puṇatambe. Three days later, he was in the entourage of Mahāyogi Cāngadev, and he was certain that this visit would vindicate the claim he had always made!

The procession was really grand. Hundreds of disciples blowing conches and slogans of '*Jai Gurudev*' in front; Yogi Cāngadev riding the back of a caparisoned tiger, with a whip of a live cobra in right hand and the *yogadaṇḍa*, a wooden armrest, in his left; and many more disciples and devotees behind him. The people were joining them at every village out of curiosity at what was to come out of this meeting of the *greats*!

At that time, the Quartet was sitting on a dilapidated wall near Iṅdrāyaṇi, happily enjoying Nature. Gangādhar came in a hurry to bring the news of Cāngadev's entourage in the outskirts of the town. Nivṛttināth looked at Jñānadev meaningfully, Sopāndev just sat silently without any reaction and Muktāyi laughed and said: "At last, we are about to meet the great *yogi*!"

Jñānadev said, looking at Gangādhar: "*Kākā*, we too should receive him with all honour!"

Patting the wall with affection, he said, "*Cal bhinti*, let us go, wall!!"

And lo behold! The wall started moving briskly towards the grand procession and met it. Cāngadev, who saw this wonder of wonders, was truly humbled. He had only brought the tiger and cobra, which were alive, under his control, but these children had the elements including a lifeless wall under their control. He literally jumped off the tiger, freeing the cobra from his hand, to rush towards these divine children. There were tears in the old man's eyes and remorse in his voice when he said: "Forgive me, forgive my arrogance and forgive my ignorance of your greatness!"

He fell prostrate and Jñānadev climbed down the wall to take him in his warm embrace. There were tears of love in Jñānadev's eyes, of strange ecstasy in Cāngadev's, and of joy in the crowd's! Cāngadev fell at Nivṛttināth's feet, who lifted him. And Sopān and Muktāyi touched Cāngadev's feet. He became emotional when he looked into the eyes of Muktāyi. Cāngadev said with all appreciation and affection: "*Māyi*, I am blessed to have your *darśana*! I have so much to learn from all of you!" So saying, he joined his palms in salutation.

Muktāyi said smilingly: "Now that you have come, all our doubts will be dissolved in Viṭṭhala!" There was so much love oozing out of her that Cāngadev remembered his forgotten mother and felt as though she had come back to him through this child! One more ecstatic person and this time it was a *yogi*, who joined the movement, with all his disciples and devotees! Muktāyi took upon herself the responsibility of one more child to her swelling number of children! She made Cāngadev understand that all the *siddhis* are only distractions for the real purpose of the realisation of being one with the cosmos. Since he had been fixated in *siddhis*, the Quartet had used them only to attract his attention and to free him from his obsession on *siddhis*!

One more apparently strong person who was very much disturbed by the event was Visobāpant. Flabbergasted, and extremely repentant for his past actions, he took the whole blame for the suffering of the family that had now become the apple of the eye of Āḷandi. When he broke down in front of the Quartet and literally rolled on the ground, Jñānadev raised him from the ground and embraced him after wiping the stream of tears that kept rolling on his old cheeks. Jñānadev said in all compassion and love: "Visobā *Kākā*, do not take the burden of blame on your shoulders. You were only a character in this great play of Existence! *Rāmāyaṇa* would not have happened, but for the role of Kaikeyi, who was instrumental in Śri Rāmā's exile! Because of you, we are what we are today. Trust us, we have nothing but respect and love for you! Do you know that we were nurtured by *Āyi* and Namu all along, which gave us plenty of time for our *sādhanā*?"

Visobā looked at Sītābāī and Namu, who were never far from the Quartet, in grateful affection. In a trice, the gap got filled as if it was never there!

The rapturous *abhaṅgs* of Nāmdev had become a favourite topic of discussion among the pilgrims returning from Pandharpur. Nivṛttināth felt that it was time for them to make that pilgrimage to Pandharpur. The group consisted of the Quartet, Cāngadev, Govind and his mother, Gangādhar Śāstri, Visobāpant, Sītābāī, Namu and a few others. Gorā Kumbhār had heard of both Nāmdev and Nivṛttināth and his siblings, all of whom were devotees. The news of the Quartet making the pilgrimage to Pandharpur travelled faster to Satyapuri and Gorobā! He called Saṅti and said with all enthusiasm: "Saṅti, it is time to fulfil our aspiration of making the pilgrimage to Pandharpur. Nivṛttināth, Jñānadev, Sopāndev and Muktābāi will be there."

Calling *Sāvaḷā* he said: "*Sāvaḷ*ā, let us go on the pilgrimage to Pandharpur, both of you get ready!"

Sāvaḷā responded in all humility: "What will we do there? Moreover, who will look after the potter-wheel business?"

When Gorā looked into the smiling eyes and faces of *Sāvaḷā* and *Sāvḷi*, he did not feel like persuading them. He just said, "As Pāṇḍuraṅga wishes!"

Quartet and devotees reached Pandharpur one evening and Gorobā with his wife reached a little earlier. They had the *darśana* of Lord Pāṇḍuraṅga and Rakhumādevi. Just in front of the sanctum sanctorum, they were attracted to a venerable person standing and singing in a very sweet voice:

'Tīrtha, holy river is Viṭṭhala, kṣetra, holy place is Viṭṭhala;
God is Viṭṭhala, the worship of God is Viṭṭhala.
Mother is Viṭṭhala, father is Viṭṭhala; relative is Viṭṭhala, lineage is Viṭṭhala.
Guru is Viṭṭhala, Gurudevatā is Viṭṭhala; temporal is Viṭṭhala, eternal is Viṭṭhala.
Nāma says he has found his Viṭṭhala; that is why times of Kaḷi, have no effect on us.'[60]

Nāmdev said, looking at all the devotees sitting there: "Let us start chanting *Viṭṭhala...Viṭṭhala...Viṭṭhala* by raising and clapping with both hands."

There was great energy, joy and ecstasy in the audience. Gorobā felt and knew the person in front dancing with *ektāri* and *ciplyā* was Viṭṭhala, the whole audience surrounding him was Viṭṭhala, and even the sweet *abhaṅg* was Viṭṭhala! Nivṛttināth and his siblings felt and shared Gorobā's experience! Saṅti, sitting next to her beloved husband, saw him raising the stumps of his hands and get immersed in the

---

60. तीर्थ विट्ठल, क्षेत्र विट्ठल। देव विट्ठल, देवपूजा विट्ठल।। १।।
माता विट्ठल, पिता विट्ठल। बन्धू विट्ठल, गोत्र विट्ठल।। २।।
गुरु विट्ठल, गुरु देवता विट्ठल। निधन विट्ठल, निरन्तर विट्ठल।। ३।।
नामा म्हणे माझा विट्ठल सापडला। म्हणूनी कळिकाळी पाड नाही।। ४।।

ecstatic chanting. As she kept on looking at him, wonder of wonders, the stumps started growing into healthy hands! Gorobā continued to chant and clap his hands.

When the chanting stopped, Saṅti's shrill voice continued the Viṭṭhala strain for awhile, and then with her eyes fixed on the image of Viṭṭhala, she entreated in a piteous voice: "O Viṭṭhala, you gave back my husband's hands after totally taking him in. Please return my only child, which you took for gracing him with your *bhakti*!"

Gorobā was too awestruck at these events to react, but he saw *Sāvaḷā* and *Sāvḷi* in place of the images of Viṭṭhala-Rakhumāyī! Just then the potter couple heard the cry of a child and Saṅti felt a tug on her sari. To their consternation, they saw their son! Both of them approached Nāmdev and fell prostrate in all gratefulness. Nāmdev was embarrassed and muttered: "No, no! It was Viṭṭhala alone who is responsible for whatever happened!"

Gorobā said in all humility: "We do understand that Viṭṭhala is behind everything that happens, but He came to us through your voice!"

Muktāyi went near them and took the child in her arms, which started smiling and playing with her. Nivṛttināth, Jñānadev, Sopāndev fell at the feet of Gorobā, who just muttered *Pāṇḍuraṅga ... Pāṇḍuraṅga,* joining his hands in salutation. When Nāmdev looked at this scene, he was curious to know about these persons. Someone whispered that they were the Āḷandi Quartet and he was Gorā Kumbhār with his wife and child.

Nāmdev looked at the four divine children much younger to him. He had never felt it before; he experienced a slight spasm of jealousy. Overriding it by chanting Viṭṭhala, he approached them. All of them fell at his feet without hesitation. Jñānadev said in all sincerity and affection: "We had heard so much about you but only today we could meet and listen to your divine *abhaṅg*. Blessed you are Nāmdevji; it is Viṭṭhala alone who is singing through you. Your birth has been a great boon to the society."

Nāmdev smiled and reacted, unable to hide the pride swelling in his breast: "What you say is right! Viṭṭhala came to me without any effort on my part. All I did was to call with my heart and being!"

Jñānadev responded: "Nāmdevji, do you think it is easy to call Him with all your being? One needs Viṭṭhala's grace to even turn one's mind towards Him!"

"I know only one thing and that is – I have accepted *Him* as my very own, my dearest friend!"

Jñānadev smiled sadly, for Nāmdev did not understand the spirit behind what was said! Muktāyi saw this and said spontaneously to everyone in general but to Nāmdev in particular: "We are in presence of a person who received the grace of Pāṇḍuraṅga in front of our very eyes! Let us take his blessings."

Gorobā responded in all humility: "I am only a potter who has received help from the greatest potter!" He laughed heartily and continued in the same jovial mood: "What can I offer the *abhaṅg śiromaṇi*, a jewel among *abhaṅ*g singers and *Jñāna* Māvuli?"

Muktāyi said with a smile: "Gorobā *Kākā*, you have been a great potter and you were helped by Pāṇḍuraṅga Himself, in your work. You must test all of us and tell us whether we are moving in the proper direction."

Immediately, Nāmdev reacted impatiently: "How can anyone possibly gauge our spiritual growth?"

Muktāyi responded patiently: "Nāmdevji, body-mind is a combination of the five elements, in which the clay component is quite predominant. Gorobā *Kākā* will be able to tell us whether we are properly baked or still incomplete."

Nāmdev could not hide his impatience: "I have other things to do than to involve myself in play."

Nivṛttināth said with a smile: "Nāmdevji, what you said

is very true, it is a play! What harm is there if the devotees of Pāṇḍuraṅga spend some time in play. After all, Viṭṭhala is no less a player than, a singer, a *jñāni* and also a *yogi*! We all are *His* children!"

Unable to say anything, Nāmdev kept silent. They sat in a line when Gorobā took out his small bamboo stick with which he checked the extent of cure in a pot! They sat in a row happily but not Nāmdev, who did not like what was going on. He sat at the end of the line reluctantly! Gorobā came near Nivṛttināth and touched his head with the stick. After listening to the sound, he commented: "It has baked totally. The pot has the complete storage of *yogic* and mystic tradition. I do not see any knower, but a vast expanse of light. It does not need any more curing.

Approaching Jñānadev, he repeated the gesture, his eyes filled and throat choked with emotion. He managed to say: "Ah! I see an ocean without any boundaries; an ocean of light, of love...infinite love. It is not love for someone or something but pure love! The light that is seen is of wisdom! I am blessed indeed to test this pot!"

Recovering, Gorobā then went near Sopāndev and touched his stick. His comment was: "This is a unique pot, fully baked! It is filled with *icchāśakti,* will and *tapas*. But the will has merged with God – God in *dhyāna*, peaceful, silent and unmoving!" It was Muktāyi's turn to offer her head to test!

Gorobā started laughing without any reason when he touched her head with his stick. He said amidst joyful laughter: "An eternal child, playful, always helpful, I see the same ocean of light and love. The ocean however is alive and moving, taking the whole universe in its bosom, caring, nurturing it with motherly love. *Māyi*...you have come to guide those on the path. Whatever actions flow through you are of great help."

Had he paid attention, Nāmdev would have understood the purpose of this play. Instead, he ran out of his patience! Gorobā hit his head with the stick and commented rather sadly: "Only this pot is not yet ready; it is still half-baked!"

Nāmdev left the temple in an obvious display of covert temper. Gorobā said, compassion obvious in his tone: "Poor Nāmdev! How close is Pāṇḍuraṅga to him, but how distant is Nāmdev!"

The group of *bhaktas* sat on the banks of Caṅdrabhāgā, just being in bliss with one another's company. Everything was in harmony and balance, the sacred river joining them through her gurgle of acceptance. It was at this point of time that Jñānadev heard a very sweet female voice singing what was so much in tune with their mood:

> '*Meditating on the name of Viṭhobā; one should take a step.*
> *Name is a great saviour; name has saved many.*
> *Ajāmiḷa was redeemed; it took Cokhāmeḷā towards salvation.*
> *Take the name while grinding and husking; says Nāmā's Jani.*'[61]

He looked at the source of this *abhaṅg* to find a lady filling a pot of water. There was so much joy in that small act that Jñānadev felt that he should go and meet her. However, as he went near her, she started walking towards the town. It was obvious that she was not conscious of anyone or anything but for her Viṭhobā! Being attracted by one of their own kind, Jñānadev, Nivṛttināth, Sopāndev and Muktāyi followed her. The lady entered a house and disappeared!

When they entered the house, they were pleasantly surprised to see Nāmdev sitting in deep thought. But the moment he saw them, he burst out in tears and said: "Forgive me Viṭṭhala. I saw you only in one form! My intimacy with you made me egoistic! Please forgive me!" So saying, he bent low joining his palms in salutation.

Jñānadev said, love and understanding oozing out of his being: "We know that Viṭṭhala never forsakes his devotees.

---

61. नाम विठोबाच घ्याव। मग पाउल टाकाव।। १।। नाम तारक हे थोर। नाम तारिले अपार।। २।। आजामेळ उद्धरिला। चोखामेळा मुक्तीस नेला।। ३।। नाम दळण कांडण। म्हणे नामयाची जनी।। ४।।

It is only a little forgetfulness on our part that makes us go astray. But His hand is always there."

Nāmdev was more than consoled. He eagerly wanted to entertain his valued guests. But Jñānadev stopped him to say: "We saw one venerable saint enter this house. We want to meet her."

Nāmdev said in all enthusiasm: "O, you mean Janātāi? She is my elder sister, who looks after me like a mother! Come, she must be in the cow-shed tending the cows or in the back-yard!"

When they reached there, they saw a strange sight. Janābāi was fighting with another lady. The reason for the quarrel was that Janābāi was alleging that the lady had stolen her dried cow-dung cakes, while the lady was claiming that they were hers! They saw them fight. When Janābāi saw Nāmdev, she asked him: "Nāma, settle our quarrel!"

Nāmdev smilingly told her: "*Tāi*, I have brought the most eligible persons with me for this work. Jñānobā! You be the judge."

With a smile, Jñānadev came near and asked: "Janātāi, all the cakes look alike; how can you differentiate them?"

Janābāi said without any hesitation: "Come hold this cake and shake it."

When Jñānadev did so, she continued: "What do you hear?"

Jñānadev heard 'Viṭṭhala... Viṭṭhala... Viṭṭhala..." with every shake!

She said: "In every move, Viṭṭhala is there! If you take any other cake that is not mine, it will not have His name!"

All of them fell at the feet of Janābāi to take her blessings. As she was looking at all of them with wonder, Janābāi exclaimed: "O Viṭṭhala... you are so playful, so wonderful! Now you are falling at my feet, taking all these forms!" She had uttered the great Truth so simply and effectively.

How true! It was Viṭṭhala who was the *Iśṭa.* He had become the *bhaktas,* and it was Viṭṭhala again who was engaged in *bhakti* in His eternal play!

When the Quartet decided to go on a pilgrimage, Nāmdev decided to join them. They started with Nasik to visit the sacred *jyotirlinga,* symbol of *Śiva, Triambakeśvar*. All the places got transformed into real sacred places of pilgrimage, as they not only visited the temples, but filled their vibrations of *bhakti* – compassion, love for nothing in particular, but the Existence in general!

Thus, the gathering that had happened at Pandharpur, went around, spreading the fragrance of love in the world!

□

11
Glimpses (*Anubhavāmṛta*) and Being

An atmosphere of balance, intimacy, brotherhood and bliss was created wherever they went. Their mission of spreading the fragrance of the spirit had commenced at Pandharpur. No one could persuade Janābāi to come with them for she had told them that Nāmā was enough to represent Viṭhobā! Gorobā Kumbhār and Saṅti with her son had stayed back at Satyapuri. Nāmdev, Cāngadev and the Quartet had sanctified most of Maharashtra. This campaign had not only helped the people and their places, but also the pilgrims in the sense that their hearts had expanded with empathy and sympathy; their understanding of the suffering of the people due to ailments like greed, infatuation, desire, anger, jealousy and pride had been confirmed; and the chanting and singing the glory of God to be a cure for these ailments was getting established.

The pilgrimage was almost coming to an end. Jñānadev had turned twenty and for almost five years the Quartet and Nāmdev had immersed themselves in the act of sharing their being with whoever came into their contact, without any discrimination whatsoever. Āḷandi was nearly a day away on foot. It was evening when they entered a hamlet, where only twenty families lived. The eyes fell on a small place of worship under a huge banyan. It was twilight and thousands of birds perched on its branches, making a great noise.

Approaching the tree, Jñānadev fell prostrate in front of the clay image of Pāṇḍuraṅga and addressed: "You are everywhere, Viṭṭhala!" The others who joined him felt that the image responded in benediction!

Jñānadev sang:

'*One who chants the name of Hari is indeed rare; Rāmakṛṣṇa is easy on speech.*
Nama Rāmakṛṣṇa achieved unmani – *transcendence of mind;*
through it crossed all siddhis.
Haripāṭh brought siddhi, buddhi *and* dharma; *covered the world in the company of saints.*
Nama Rāmakṛṣṇa has enveloped Jñānadev;
can feel atmārāma *in all ten directions.*'[62]

It was Nāmdev's turn to contribute to the milieu, he sang:

'*While sitting, sleeping, eating and going;*
may my mind be with your lotus feet.
You alone can destroy the dirt of saṁsāra;
night and day be with me.
Living in the mind of bhakta-s *as meditation;*
O protector of cattle, be with us, orphans.
Nāmā says sarvottamā *listens to name alone; God, please relieve me of burden of* saṁsāra.'[63]

The whole group merged as one to spread the fragrance of love and compassion, of wisdom that all so-called

62. हरिनाम जपे तो नर दुर्लभ। वाचेसी सुलभ रामकृष्ण।। १।।
राम कृष्ण नात उन्मनी साधली। तयासी लाधली सकळ सिध्दी।। २।।
सिध्दी बुध्दि धर्म हरिपाठ आले। प्रपंची निवाले साधुसंगे।। ३।।
ज्ञानदेवा नाम रामकृष्ण ठसा। येण दशदिशा आत्माराम।। ४।।

63. आसन शयन भोजन गमन। तुझे पाय दोन्ही दावी मझ।। १।।
संसार कल्मश समूळ छेदिसी। दाव अहर्निश पाय मझ।। २।।
हरि ध्यान मन भक्तां तूं परेशा। अनाथ का वसा गा वळियां।। ३।।
नामा म्हणे नाम ऐका सर्वोत्तमा। संसारिचा श्रमा वार देवा।। ४।।

differentiation is just appearance born out of forgetfulness. They were convinced that God had always been with them but their eyes were looking elsewhere! How could they ever miss Him? It had been so obvious that they had taken Him for granted!

Yogi Cāngadev, Gangādhar, Govind, Bhāmātāi, Sītābāī, Namu, Visobā and others felt blessed. All the strain of the journey was eliminated. Though they had no food that day, who cared as Viṭhobā occupied their being in presence of the Quartet and Nāmdev? The next day when they reached Āḷandi, it was in a festive mood. The town was decorated with festoons, garlands and delightful smiles adorning the faces of all occupants, young and old! Nāmdev, Nivṛttināth, Jñānadev, Sopāndev, Muktāyi accepted the warmth from the people through the reception offered to them. Nāmdev sang a few *abhaṅgs* and demonstrated the effortlessness of *nāmasmaraṇam*, when everyone started chanting *Jai Jai Rāmakṛṣṇa Hari*!

Nivṛttināth observed Jñānadev remaining non-involved in the external proceedings as his attention was totally inward towards his being. He knew that time for Jñānadev's withdrawal from the world was approaching.

Early next morning, Nāmdev came to the tree where the Quartet was sitting silently in bliss. He sat near Jñānadev and said: "Jñānadev, I can never free myself from your debt."

Jñānadev was surprised at this and said with bliss in his being: "Nāmdevji, what have I given you? Moreover, all of us have gained much from your *sādhu saṅga*."

But Nāmdev was in tears when he rejoined: "No *Devā*, I was so conceited as to think myself to be the only friend of Viṭhobā! I feel that still I have much to learn. Tell me what should I do?"

Jñānadev looked at Nivṛttināth, who nodded. Then he said with all love and affection: "Nāmdevji, it is Viṭṭhala alone who is playing different roles through us. We have definite roles to play and we all are playing our roles perfectly *as* He wants us to! You have to complete your role of this life. It seems Viṭṭhala wants to sing many more *abhaṅgs* through you. Continue your pilgrimage and spread the path of love. Many are there, waiting for you to quench their thirst. Go into the world and be the bard of *vārakaris*!"

Nāmdev left, taking a tearful leave. The Quartet saw his receding figure slowly diminishing, which they knew would spread and envelop the world.

Finding Jñānadev alone, Nivṛttināth came near to talk to him: "Jñānā, I see a change in you. Tell me about it."

Jñānadev touched his feet and said: "*Dādā*, I feel my work now is finished!"

Nivṛttināth was not surprised. He said solemnly: "I knew this the day before when the town was in celebration. But must you withdraw?"

Jñānadev had tears, but they had pure bliss and gratefulness behind them. He said: "*Dādā*, when Māvuli *Ātmā* calls, can you play deaf ears to her?! All along I used to call her. But now, she is calling me, and I possibly cannot resist!"

Nivṛttināth responded: "I do understand, but before withdrawal, will you do something for our *nāth sampradāya*?"

Jñānadev got up and prostrated, saying with his ever-ready tears: "*Dādā*, just command me; you have been my Creator and whatever I am, is only due to your grace and blessings."

"Jñānā, *Bhāvārthadīpikā* is on the song of the Lord. Govind and others have recorded your *abhaṅgs*. You have had experiences after living the teachings of our *Nāth sampradāya*. Time is now ripe for writing about them to help the present and future seekers."

"As you wish, Gurudev."

Jñānadev retreated to the tree under which they had spent most of their time in their *sādhanā*. He could still feel the spiritual vibrations; could hear the voice of his beloved brother and *guru*, talking to him about the *sampradāya* of Gorakṣanāth; about the axioms upon which the whole practice depends, the practices themselves which have been transferred from the *gurus* to their *śiṣyas*. It was as though the whole current of tradition passed in front of his very senses. All Jñānadev did was to become silent and totally relaxed to tune into his being.

As Jñānadev sought the blessings of his *guru paramparā*, he saw Ādi Guru Gorakṣanāth and felt his hand on the head. The visual vibrations of lineage of preceptors the great tradition of Nāth flashed through his being, showering their benediction. Then Jñānadev felt the blissful presence of his *guru*, his own dear brother Nivṛttināth in his heart. Reassured, he continued to delve within to touch the origin: Infinite, Eternal, silent ocean of consciousness. It could not even be called ocean as there was neither *draśṭā* - seer nor *dṛśya* – scene. Words failed, and nor did Jñānadev seek any description, but merged blissfully!

A while later, a feeling of self-love arose from within, and Śakti*, the tendency to vibrate and move,* rose amidst Śiva, the silence. Śakti in turn felt the need to see the formless *Śiva* and she covered His being with the multi-coloured robe[64] of the universe. The presence of the third entity however, did not intrude upon their unity and no-otherness. Jñānadev was not separate from this wonderful phenomenon as he had totally dissolved his puny ego into the ocean. Through this experience, Jñānadev understood the process of creation and dissolution.

Jñānadev went into ecstasy as he dwelt on the *guru* without whose grace, nothing is possible. *Guru* hastens the progress of the disciple. *Guru* does not make any distinction between great and small while pouring his grace through liberation. Preceptor makes all-out efforts to ensure that the disciple's illusion of multiplicity and hence the ignorance and even his knowledge (the binding thought of *I-know*) is destroyed. The *guru* does not differentiate between himself

64. Jñānadev uses this metaphor to describe the universe which has formed out of the same ocean of consciousness. Spiritual practices of *Nāth paramparā* and subsequent *bhakti* movement are based on this *no-otherness* of universe and God.

and the disciple, as he is always *in no-otherness*. By taking shelter and totally surrendering oneself at the feet of such *guru*, all doubts are dissolved and debt of human birth is cleared. Jñānadev gratefully remembered the grace of Lord for making such a *guru* available to him in his own elder brother.

Speech happens to be the most important obstacle that binds due to illusion, as well as the means through which liberation is achieved! However, speech is not only the activity of the tongue but the involvement with the *external* through the body, senses and with the *internal* through *manas* and *buddhi.*[65] Though one starts with *nāmasmaraṇam* – the act of remembering with help of chanting of name, it takes one deeper into self through the grace of *guru* who makes the disciple aware of the unity of the name, *smaraṇam* and the one who is remembering! It is *guru* again, who holds the hand of his disciple and protects when the disciple is walking through the sticky mire of *Tripuṭi* – the triad of known, knowing and knower (*jñeya—jñāna—jñātṛ*), object, experience and experiencer (*bhojyam-bhogam-bhoktā*) and act, action and actor (*karya-karma-kartā*).

Remembering his experience of the reality, Jñānadev remembered that being in reality is not really an experience! And that *sat* – absolute Existence, *cit* – absolute wisdom and *ānaṅda* – absolute bliss are only three consequences of being in reality! They really are the three guiding attributes or words to denote Him who transcends all description! *Ātma* Māvuli is self-evident and does not need any assistance, including the words for proving its Existence. The Sun (reality) never meets darkness (ignorance), hence is called the enemy of darkness! Actually, the absence of sun is darkness! Turning one's face from light is darkness! Guru Nivṛttināth had helped Jñānadev transcend the duality of knowledge and ignorance and to know that all the activity was just happening without being conscious of either activity or actor! At the end of his narration of the *Anubhavāmṛta – glimpses into being*, Jñānadev

---

65. वागत्रोपलक्षणार्था सर्वेन्द्रियाणम्।। कठोपनिषद् शंकरभाष्यम् १.३.१३।।

invoked the blessings for all Existence from the Lord through *pasāyadāna* – gift of *Divine* grace:

'Now O Lord of the universe,
accept this offering, knit out of words.
Accepting thus, grant me pasāyadāna *your gift of Divine grace.*
May the evil shed their wickedness, may their attraction for good deeds enhance.
May all living beings be linked by the bond of kinship.
May the darkness enveloping the ignorant, pass.
May the universe be lit by the sun of conscious divinity ever present in every being.
May every being get what it needs.
Inundate everyone with your grace.
May the world be filled by those
who trust in the goodness of the Divine.
May these beings overflowing with love,
meet ceaselessly.
May the world be spread with groves of wish-fulfilling trees.
May there be colonies of radiant Cintāmaṇi of consciousness.
May these enlightened wise speak words,
sweet like heaven's nectar.
May these persons be like the moon
without spots and the sun without heat.
May those who are kind to all discover their love for you.
May the people in all three planes, be content and gratified in all ways.
May they perpetually sing the glories of Ādi Puruṣa,
the original being.
May those who follow and live these scriptures meticulously, guide others.
May they find victory over the seen and the unseen.
And this O Lord of the universe,
Will be the most charitable gift – the
gift of divine grace.

And this made Jñānadev happy, content and blissfull.'[66]

As he kept this work at the feet of his beloved brother and *guru*, after washing the feet with his tears of gratefulness, Jñānadev felt fulfilled. The eyes of Nivṛttināth were also filled with tears of love and intimacy. He knew that now the Lord had freed Jñānadev of all responsibilities in this life. He asked him in all affection: "Jñānā, I know it is difficult to resist the *call*. But it is only appropriate that we should meet those who have helped us in our life and celebrate togetherness before you withdraw. When do you propose to take *samādhi*?"

Jñānadev closed his eyes to dive within before responding a little later: "Gurudev, thirteenth day of the dark fortnight of the sacred month of *Kārtik*,[67] would be ideal for withdrawal."

Sopāndev heard this conversation between his two elder brothers. It could not be really called reaction, but nor was it a response! His Jñāndādā had been with him all through his life, from birth to this day, sharing his negative as well as the positive experiences. There was a concern: 'without him, will the life be the same?' But out of nowhere came a thought, strong as the suggestions he had received from his dear Jñāndādā: 'how can you *part from the one who lives in your heart*?' It acted like a refreshing breeze on a hot summer day; like the sweet warmth of the hearth on a cold winter night; and like the sight of cascade of water and bounty of flowers and fruits in a desert! He felt at ease with his self and the surroundings.

Muktāyi was her usual calm, happy and boisterous self, making all the arrangements for her dearest Jñān *Dādā's*

---

66. आतां विश्वात्मके देवे। येणे वाग्यज्ञे तोषावे। तोषोनि मज़ द्यावे पसायदान हे।। १।। जेखळांची व्यंकटी सांडो। तया सत्कर्मीं रती वाढो। भूतां परस्परे जडो। मैत्र जीवांचे।। २।। दुरितांचे तिमिर ज़ावो। विश्वस्वधर्मसूर्ये पाहो। जो जे वांच्छिल तो ते लाहो। प्राणिजात।। ४।। वर्षत सकळ मंगळी। ईश्वरनिष्ठांची मांदियाळी। अनवरत भूमंडळी। भेटो तया भूतां।। ५।। चला कल्पतरुंचे आरव। चेतना चिंतामणीचे गाव। बोलते जे ते अर्णव। पियुषांचे।। ६।। चंद्रमे जे अलांच्छन। मार्तंड जे तापहीन। ते सर्वाही सदा सज्जन। सोइरे होतु।। ७।। किं बहुना सर्व सुखी। पूर्ण होउनि तिही लोकी। भजिजे आदिपुरुखी। अखंडित।। ८।। आणि ग्रंथोपजीविये। विशेषी लोकी इये। दृष्टादृष्ठ विजये। होवावे जी।। ९।। येथ म्हणे श्रीविश्वेश्वरावो। हा होईल दान पसावो। येणे वरे ज्ञानदेवो सुखिया जाहला।। १०।।
67. 2 December, 2021 was the 725th year of Sanjīvana Samādhi of Saṅt Jñānadev.

Sanjīvana samādhi. She felt that though she had missed running around in managing the *yajñopavit* ceremonies of her brothers, God was giving her the opportunity for a much bigger event! Cāngadev was with her all along to be of some help.

Sītābāī, Namu and Visobā felt as though their Jñānadev was being snatched away. So were Govind, Gangādhar, Bhāmātāi, Vidyādhar and others who had tasted the nectar of Jñānadev's divine company. They all sat near the sacred tree, concerned about their own future. The others who had joined this sacred assemblage were crestfallen. They had gained so much in so little time, and yet the person who had been responsible for this boon would be leaving them for good, soon. Though it was a natural reaction Dhoṅdu *Kākā* was an exception. Noting the expressions on their faces, he came near them and started speaking: "Why is there sadness instead of joy in this time of celebration?"

Govind replied gravely: "*Kākā,* don't you realise, Māvuli is being snatched away from us? Our motherly *guru* who knew and understood every little feeling in us will be no more with us."

They were surprised when Dhoṅḍu *Kākā* laughed and said in a tone of admonition: "*Deva* is with us now! Make best use of the time now, there is ample time now, then why are you worried and concerned about when he will not be? Get up and be near Māvuli and harvest love and joy!"

All the so-called scholars and their companions shook away the negative feelings to seek their Jñāneśwar Māvuli!

News reached all the *bhaktas* and they started arriving at Āḷandi as quickly as possible. Yogi Cāngadev had never left the shelter of his mother and Guru Muktāyi. Gorā Kumbhār and Saṅti reached well in time. During that time, Nāmdev was in a neighbouring state. It was late evening when he heard the news. Nāmdev was no doubt shaken, but he could never miss such a great opportunity to have the last *darśana* of his dearest friend, his guide and companion in the pilgrimage, and one of his *gurus*, who had pointed and made him see the *cosmic* God. He started his journey forthwith and hurried towards Āḷandi. Once again, the birds of the same feather of *bhakti* gathered and the celebration of Divine name and the feast of togetherness began. Gorobā could not contain his joy on seeing Nāmdev arrive at Āḷandi. He saw infinite love oozing out of Nāmdev's being. A spontaneous *abhaṅg* came through:

> *'Attribute-less came to meet the attribute; with you I transcended all attributes.*
> *Since I don't have any form, how can there be any name? I have become speechless!*
> *As I tried to speak the tongue went backwards;* khecari[68] *happened without any effort!*
> *Gorā Kumbhār says meeting you Nāmdev, how did this embrace of bliss happen?'*[69]

They walked towards the tree to meet Nivṛttināth, Jñānadev, Sopāndev and others. Nāmdev ran and fell at their feet. Jñānadev held him in a warm embrace that cleared all concern and sadness from his heart. As Jñānadev spoke looking towards Nāmdev, they all experienced bliss – the joy without reason!

"Nāmdevji, please bless this assembly with your *nāma garjana* – roar of name!" When the command was from Jñānadev, how could he possibly resist, so started Nāmdev closing his eyes:

> *'The roar of name resonates on the banks of Bhīmā;*
> *Listen to your greatness in those voices.*
> *Your servants* riddhi-siddhi *(the Divine powers) are sweeping the courtyard;*
> *The four efforts* – dharma, artha, kāma *and* mokṣa *are*

---

68. *Khecari* is a *yogic mudrā* when the tip of the tongue closes the throat for one who experiences *samādhi*.

69. निर्गुणाचें भेटी आलों सगुणासंगे। तंव झालो प्रसंगी गुणातीत।। १।।
मज रूप नाही नांव सांगू काई। झाला बाई काई बोलूं नये।। २।।
बोलतां आपुली जिव्हा पैं खादली। खेचरी लागली पाहता पाहता।। ३।।
म्हणे गोरा कुंभार नाम्या तुझी भेटी। सुखासुखी मिठी पडली कैसी।। ४।।

cleaning the remains of your food.
The four Vedas *are roaring having become your announcers;*
Sanat Kumara-s and other sages are singing your glories.
Gods are rolling in your courtyard;
Śiva is taking the dust of your lotus feet.
Nāmā says may the grace of Deva,
who looks after all, be on this Existence.'[70]

After a while, Jñānadev remembered the pilgrimage and expressed it to the group: "We had gone on a blissful pilgrimage to the sacred *tīrthas* that are outside. Our gathering was so fruitful to become not only memories of our lifetime, but also to the pilgrims of future. During our journey we had also gone within to feel *His* presence in our being. Now the time is ripe for us to take that pilgrimage inside together."

"*Devā,* tell us of your own journey." It was Gangādhar Śāstri who expressed the wish of others.

Jñānadev sought the permission by turning his eyes towards his *guru*. Nivṛttināth nodded in response: '*The wisdom of unblemished perfection surpasses all knowledge;*

I received this on serving yogirāj *(Nivṛttināth).*
Renouncing the attachment to the physical
I acquired this wisdom;
And that has given me great contentment and poise.
Non-attachment has dissolved the inherent imperfection of māyā, *the temporal world;*
I perceive the ever-present true inner essence.
The cosmic Aśwattha *tree (illusionary world) has bloomed with sandalwood fragrance;*
Likewise, I have seen the formless one in this illusory world.
Enough of this prapañca *– world of five elements;*
I would like to be, to remain in self.

---

70. नामाचा गजर गर्जे भीमातीर। महिमा साजे थोर तुज एका।। १।।
ऋद्धि सिद्धि दासी अंगण झाडती। उच्छिष्ठे काडती मुक्ति चारी।। २।।
चारी वेद भाट होऊनी गर्जती। सनकादिक गाती कीर्ती तुझी।। ३।।
सुरवरांचे भार अंगणी लोळती। चरणरज क्षिती शिव वंदी।। ४।।
नामा म्हणे देव ऐसा हो कृपाळू। करितो संभाळु अनाथांचा।। ५।।

I have found shelter in Viṭṭhala
the companion of Rakhumādevi, the ocean of wisdom.'[71]

The togetherness of seekers and saints spread waves of *bhakti* in and around Āḷandi. No one realised the passage of time, and thirteenth day of the dark fortnight of *Kārtik* arrived. Arrangements for the feast for the whole village and its guests were made. On hearing the news of Jñānadev's exit, many new faces had arrived there. Some of them were genuine seekers, others were the persons who had heard of the divine powers of Jñānadev, and some others were just curious onlookers!

Very early that morning, Nivṛttināth, Jñānadev and Sopāndev sat near Mother Iṅdrāyaṇi, to be in communion with her. They had spent much of their time with her and she had played a distinct role in their physical as well as spiritual growth. While Nivṛttināth and Jñānadev were full and flowing like the river in front of them, Sopān was getting upset. His inability to withhold the emotions forced him to pour out: "Jñāndādā, must you go?"

The elder brother in Jñānadev was evoked as he said affectionately: "Sopān, *Baḷ*, who told you about going? I am not going anywhere! I will be here always."

Surprised by the statement, he was unable to believe his ears! He burst out: "So, you are not leaving after all!"

With all affection Jñānadev continued: "Sopān, whoever enters this material world has to leave his physical frame one day or the other. But it does not really mean that he leaves the world altogether. Our great *sampradāya* has this tradition of *sañjīvana samādhi*. Though one who takes it will not be there in body, he will remain *in essence.* Those eligible seekers who are in need of any spiritual guidance will get it through him.

71. अधिक देखणे तरि निरंजन पाहणे। योगिराज विनावण मना आल वो माये।।
देहबळि देऊनी साधिल म्यां साधन। तेणे समाधान मज जोडल वो माये।। १।।
अनंगपण फिटल मायाछंदा सांठविल। सकळ देखिल आत्मस्वरूप वो माये।। २।।
चंदन जेव भरला अश्वत्थ फुलला। तैसा म्या देखिला निराकार वो माये।। ३।।
पुरे पुरे आतां प्रपंच पाहणे। निजानंदी राहणे स्वरूपी वो माये।। ४।।
ऐसा ज्ञानसागरू रखुमादेविवरू। विट्ठलुं निर्धारू म्यां देखिला वो माये।। ५।।

Moreover *Bāḷ*, we have learnt through our *sādhanā* and being that we are not limited to the physical alone, but are *pūrṇa* – the whole. Being the whole, how can 'I' be separate from 'you'?" So saying, Jñānadev kept his palm on the head of Sopān, who was freed from all doubt and concern.

A cave was dug near the temple of Siddheśwar. The pathway to it was decorated with festoons and flowers. After everyone had partaken of the *prasād*, the gathering assembled in front. Nivrttinath and Sopān stood on the right, Nāmdev, Gorobā and Cāngadev on the left of Jñānadev, who stood, his eyes half closed, lips wearing an ethereal smile. All persons felt that his gaze was on every being and his physical frame was losing its earthly nature! He sang the one last *abhaṅg* through his form:

> 'Samādhi *is achieved by the eternal name;*
> *Peace, compassion, equanimity and everything is only the outcome.*
> *Nivṛtti is the giver of peace of peace; he gave this panacea of chanting the name of Hari.*
> *Patience, self-control, technique of knowledge and wisdom;*
> *Never shall the ignorance return again.*
> *Jñānadev says, pursuit of* siddhis *is dangerous;*
> *Path of* bhakti *is the path to Hari.*
> Samādhi *is achieved by the eternal name;*
> *Peace, compassion, equanimity and everything is only the outcome.*'[72]

His voice had a commanding sweetness, a compassionate and eternal message and an illuminating influence on the listeners' beings. It assured them all that he had performed the penance for all the people present there at that point of time; all those who had left the world, and all those who would visit this wonderful world in future – near and far! Bending low, he looked into the eyes of his beloved brother and *guru*,

72. समाधी साधन संजीवन नाम । शान्ति दया सम सर्वांभूति ।। शान्ति ची पैशान्ति निवृत्तिदातारु। हरि नाम उच्चारू दिधला तेण, दिधला तेणें ।। शम दम कळा विज्ञान सज्ञान । परतोंनि अज्ञान न ये घरा, न ये घरा।। ज्ञानदेव सिद्धि साधना अवीट। भक्तिमार्ग नीट हरि पंथि, हरि पंथि।।

who clasped his right hand, Sopān, his left hand. Muktāyi and Nāmdev led the way into the cave. Gorobā started chanting, "*Jai Jai Rāmakṛṣṇa Hari*" with Cāngadev dancing in ecstasy.

The roar of the *name* reverberated around the Earth, the sky, to spread into the universe. Tears overflowing the eyes of the devotees blurred the form of the wonderful divine youth who had taught alchemy of emotions through the simple *nāmasmaraṇam.* And he entered the cave of eternal haven of *sat-cit-ānańda* – being-wisdom-bliss!

□

12
Resurrection

The tree had grown silent of the noise of thousands of birds enveloped by restful sleep. An occasional hoot of a night bird was only strengthening the effect of silence. A small hearth was providing warmth and light to the pilgrims from Paiṭhan. Though they could not see River Iṅdrāyaṇi, she could be heard through the steady gurgle of her movement. They would reach Āḷandi the next morning. Saṅt Ekanāth and his two companions – son Hari and Balavant Śāstry had literally meditated on Jñānadev during the past few days and nights as he had remembered and narrated the saint's glorious life. All three of them experienced no fatigue after walking the long distance. Hari wanted to know more about the three siblings of Saṅt Jñānadev.

Ekanāth looked towards the rising flames of *dhuni* – a small warmth and light giving the hearth and said with a sigh: "Sopāndev dropped his body within a month after *sanjīvana samādhi of* Jñānarāj Māvuli at Sāsvad. Muktāyi being the youngest of the divine siblings had been the apple of their eyes. Though she was extremely fond of all her elder brothers, she was devoted to Jñānadev. The departure of the two of her brothers made her more and more meditatively introvert. Guru Nivṛttināth and Muktāyi went around the different places of pilgrimage, during which Cāngadev, her disciple, expressed his wish to be allowed to withdraw from his long life. Accordingly, the ancient *yogi* who had been enlightened by his child-mother Muktāyi entered *samādhi* at Puṇtambe, the place where he had spent most of his long life. Muktāyi had brought light to Cāngadev's life and helped him to achieve *nirvāṇa.* The group of saints continued their pilgrimage to different holy places and reached a place called Mehuḷ, on the bank of River Tāpi. When the group was taking a dip in the river, it started drizzling. They heard the loud clash of thunder and saw lightning strike the very place where Muktāyi stood. When they rushed to the place, they saw her not – Muktāyi had withdrawn from the mortal world. Guru Nivṛttināth took *samādhi* at Triambakeśvar. Saṅt Nāmdev fulfilled Māvuli's wish by continuing to spread the message of *bhakti* in distant lands of Punjab[73], Haryanā and the north. This bouquet of singing saints made *a* unit, literally started the mission of *bhakti* together."

There were tears in the eyes of Ekanāth as he finished his narration. Hari and Balavant were silent as they joined Ekanāth in his offering their gratitude to the great tradition.

As his two companions slept, Ekanāth sat and continued to look at the dying flames of the *dhuni*. He thought of these great persons. They were like the fire, always moving upwards, unaffected by the daunting or favourable situations, always helpful; in spite of all the challenges, always stable; and never complaining in the face of persecutions of the contemporary society, ever understanding, compassionate and loving. The fire in front brought an insight: they are like the wood offering warmth and light when it burns! He did not realise the passage of night, until he heard the birds welcoming the dawn. His eyes fell on the sleeping son and friend – their faces innocent and trusting, and thought it better not to disturb them. Ekanāth wanted to find the place of *sanjīvana samādhi.* He enquired about it from the first person he met: "Can you please show me the *samādhi* of Jñānadev Māvuli?"

73. His *abhaṅgs* found their honourable place in *Guru Granth Sāhib*, the sacred book of the Khālsas (Sikhs).

And to his utter surprise that man did not know about Māvuli! Almost every person he met replied him in the negative. Approaching an old man sitting on the parapet of his house, he repeated the question. A question was the old man's reply: "Who is he? Never heard of him!"

Ekanāth was awestruck; he said: "More than two hundred years back, Jñānadev Mahārāj was born in this very place and spread the love of God. He took *sanjīvana samādhi* near Siddheśwar temple at a tender age of twenty-one."

The old man laughed and blurted out: "You are talking of a man who died two hundred years back! We forget our dead after the thirteenth day! About a temple, none of us has seen it! My father used to say that the original town of Āḷandi was claimed by the jungle! Anyway, what have you to do with a man who died more than two centuries back?"

Ekanāth chose to remain silent. He withdrew from the place and went back to the river. As he sat looking at the waves, alive and moving, it struck him that in that dream, Māvuli had mentioned about the roots of *Ajāna* tree strangling his throat. The *Ajāna* tree he had referred to was *Ajñāna* – ignorance and forgetfulness, and the throat was the heritage of his spoken word! Ekanāth wondered about the short memory of the people who had been living in this sacred place for centuries. But when he looked more closely at Iṅdrāyaṇi, he realised that since everything changes continually and constantly, forgetfulness is not a vice but it happens to be the helplessness of those who are overwhelmed by the change. In all gratefulness, Ekanāth bowed low to the river.

Hari and Balavant, not finding Ekanāth with them, were relieved to find him near the river. Hari asked whether his father had any clue of the saint's *samādhi*. Saṅt Ekanāth responded calmly, pointing in the direction: "Yes, it is inside the thick jungle yonder. We will start looking without losing time."

He started walking on the bank into the thick forest and they followed. They did not have any tool to cut the creepers and thorny bushes. It did not deter Ekanāth who kept walking, not caring about the thorns or obstacles. As they moved further, they came across the tall grass. Hari and Balavant lost way and were unable to follow him. Though they continued, they were clueless of Ekanāth's whereabouts. Tired and hungry, they returned to the village. Ekanāth went on remembering Māvuli and his legs kept moving till his eyes fell on a dilapidated stone structure of a temple. Hurrying towards it, he entered, clearing the webs of centuries that had covered the entrance. Seeing the stone image of Siddheśwar in the form of a *lingam*, he offered his salutations. The *samādhi* was somewhere nearby and he started going around. Though he circumambulated thrice around, he could not find any sign. He was exhausted, hungry and thirsty. But the thirst to be in *His* presence who had called him was more intense; and the very hunger to know gave him the energy to look for the *samādhi* with renewed enthusiasm. In a place he took the support of a flat stone to avoid a fall, and suddenly the stone moved and he beheld a pathway leading to the cave. Ekanāth had succeeded!

He touched his head on the threshold of the cave and slowly started climbing down the stones which had been arranged as steps. Smell of sandalwood was the first to greet his nostrils. Then his eyes beheld a soft light guiding him to the floor of the cave. The flowers – marigold, appeared fresh as though they had been kept only recently. He heard a voice, bell-like and sweet: "Come Ekanāth. I have been waiting for you!"

Ekanāth prostrated in the direction of the sound without opening his eyes. When he raised his head, he saw. It was a youth – bright, effulgent; his voice spread a feeling of joy in Ekanāth, who was speechless. The roots of the tree above did strangle his neck and throat, but there was no struggle or pain in that wonderful face!

Unable to bear the sight, Ekanāth tried to go near to free the form from the stranglehold of roots. The form smiled instead, to say: "It is not the material strangulation Ekanāth, but verbal and spiritual. You alone can relieve me from this bondage!"

Ekanāth said in all humility: "Māvuli, your words have been guiding so many in freeing themselves, how can you be possibly bound by anything?"

"Time Ekanāth, time. Man has been gifted by this boon of forgetfulness! It is a boon if he forgets the negative events of his life. Normally, he always remembers them! It becomes a bane if he loses the memory of good events having the quality of freeing us from bondage and misery. Two hundred years is not really long, but it does become so, if we are under the influence of bodily indulgence and mental involvement with the change and challenges that is life."

There was a full pause for the words to sink in. Māvuli continued: "You have been chosen by Providence to revive the great message of Truth, for which we had become conduits for manifestation. You should not entertain any doubt in your mind about your *adhikāra* – eligibility."

The moment Ekanāth heard these words, a new strength flowed in his veins and spirit. He waited almost holding his breath for the next instruction of Māvuli.

In the village, Hari and Balavant Śāstry went on searching for Saṅt Ekanāth in the forest, but failed. Concerned, Balavant offered to go back to Paiṭhan for getting help. However, in his heart he had doubts about safety of the saiṅt and was really worried about his becoming food for the wild animals. He asked Hari to keep looking and searching for his dear father and that he would return after getting help from Paiṭhan. Hari knew that his father was safe and even in this disappearance, there was some divine plan. But since there was no help from this new village of Āḷandi, he agreed to let Balavant go back to Paiṭhan for help.

Seeing Balavant Śāstry return to Paiṭhan without Saṅt Ekanāth and Hari, the whole town was worried. Everyone, —including his critics, had grown fond of this quiet saint who never showed any superiority over people, who bore whatever happened in life either due to persons or nature with equipoise and joy. They felt responsible for the safety of their town-mate, their friend and guide. And Paiṭhan got ready to proceed to Āḷandi for bringing him back.

It had been nearly four days since his father's disappearance and now Hari was really in doubt: did something happen? He did not want to entertain it and so started chanting *"Jai Jai Rāmakṛṣṇa Hari"* instead. Since his childhood, his father had been a living example of patience and equipoise. For him nothing was unbearable or unsolvable with the ever-present God within. Ekanāth used to say that prayers and worship were really meant to turn our attention to this *aṅtaryāmin* – controller within. The chanting helped him to calm his mind and nerves, while his eyes and senses became sharper and started looking for his dear father.

Inside the cave, the milieu was entirely ethereal and divine. Ekanāth was totally oblivious to the passing of days or nights and the so-called passage of time! He continued to drink the ambrosia coming out of Māvuli. The unnoticeable mistakes that had crept into *Bhāvārthadīpikā* as well as *Anubhavāmṛta* were pointed out along with their corrections. The twenty-seven *abhaṅgs* of *Haripāṭh* were sung into the being of Ekanāth for whom, Māvuli was inseparable. This grand communion in sound was followed by silence when Ekanāth felt the *jñāna* enter his being. It was a resurrection of Jñānadev Māvuli. He heard the voice once again: "Ekanāth, it is now time for you to wake up to the world of elements."

As he opened his eyes, Ekanāth saw that the Divine form no more had the strangulating roots. The right hand was raised in benediction and it started to fade and, in its place, the cave and *prapaṅca* – the material world of five elements started to manifest. Ekanāth realised that the disappearance and appearance was only the play of attention! When one is attentive to God, the world is not, and when one is attentive to the world, God is not! The voice within whispered: "Wait, don't come to a conclusion yet!"

An insight struck him like a sudden clash of lightning: "The God is not because we see Him as the world; and the world is not because we see it as God! He is Māvuli; Māvuli is I; and I am He!" Ekanāth was ecstatic, blissful and full. He started dancing. The mood continued to overflow from his being as he came out. With the same worshipful attitude, he closed the cave with the flat rock firmly as he had found it.

Just then he heard someone call: "*Bābā*!!"

It was Hari who rushed to him and fell at his feet. Ekanāth pressed him to his heart to transfer the bliss of his being. Hari spoke in all enthusiasm: "When we did not see you for days, Balavant *Kākā* returned to Paiṭhan to get some help. I have been searching for you all these days and today morning I started chanting *Rāmakṛṣṇa Hari* to get rid of unwanted thoughts! I do not know how, but I started walking in this direction and just when I came near this spot, I saw you! "*Jai Jai Rāmakṛṣṇa Hari*!"

Ekanāth responded in kind with all joy. 'How wonderful it is! The whole Existence has transformed' felt Saṅt Ekanāth.

Hari noticed that father had changed. *Bābā* was silently blissful and blissfully silent. He was certain that the purpose of coming to Āḷandi had been achieved. Hari completed his thought verbally: "*Bābā*, did you have *darśana* of Māvuli?"

In response Saṅt Ekanāth just looked into the eyes of Hari, communicating that it was more than just *darśana*; it was transfusion and transformation. Hari understood. They were approaching the bank of Iṅdrāyaṇi when they saw a very large group of persons headed by Balavant Śāstry, who was relieved to see the father and son safe. There were shouts of joy when the people from Paiṭhan beheld their saint, who continued to be as he always was: in poise, content and blissful.

Unable to restrain their curiosity in finding a large group of people from Paiṭhan in their village, the people at Āḷandi came near them. The same old man who had made fun of Ekanāth was the first to speak. There was respect in his tone as he addressed Saṅt Ekanāth: "We did not realise the gravity of your search. Now it appears we have insulted a saint, by belittling you. Please forgive us. Did you find that *samādhi*?"

Sant Ekanāth responded in kindness: "It is not your fault if Jñānadev Māvuli was erased from the memory of Āḷandi. Everything happening in this Existence has some purpose, though we may not be able to understand it. Siddheśwar temple is the heart of Āḷandi, and the *saṅjīvana samādhi* is the *ātman*. Āḷandi will become the centre for spreading the path of *bhakti* once again. Will you join your hands in rebuilding the temple and *samādhi* with us?"

As he looked around, Saṅt Ekanāth saw the new enthusiasm and energy in the eyes of his companions of Paiṭhan and Āḷandi. He had felt these very inspirations while in the cave with Māvuli. The crowd shouted in one loud voice: "*Jai Jai Rāmakṛṣṇa Hari*!"

And so it was that the process of re-building the temple began. New granite, building materials, artisans, craftsmen, masons and carpenters came from Paiṭhan. They were the descendants of the persons who had poured their affection for the Quartet when they had come for *śuddhipatra*. The farmers from Nevāsā came to help grow food in Āḷandi to feed its people and the pilgrims that were slowly gathering.

Saṅt Ekanāth started another and more important work of editing and presenting the correct versions of *Bhāvārthadīpikā* and *Anubhavāmṛta*. During the audience Ekanāth had sought consent of Māvuli, to call the work *Amṛtānubhava*, which was readily agreed upon by Māvuli. He discovered to his pleasant surprise that the persons who helped him to make the copies of these manuscripts were in tune with the teachings therein, so much so, that their lives were getting transformed. The language was so beautiful and easy that anyone could understand and live their essence.

The most beautiful development was his introducing the chanting of *Haripāṭh* as a morning and evening routine for the devotees. Saṅt Ekanāth told the devotees that if it was not possible to chant in the morning, they should do so every evening. He explained to them that whatever was in *Bhāvārthadīpikā* and *Amṛtānubhava* – the two scriptures, had been condensed by Māvuli in his infinite compassion for the common masses. Even the persons who could read and understand the scriptures found it effortless to introduce the chanting of *Haripāṭh* with total attention of mind and heart. Consequently, the society started breaking the walls of differences.

The farmers, potters, weavers, blacksmiths, as well as all the other members of the society started living as one big family of devotees of Viṭṭhala, Pāṇḍuraṅga, or the Lord of Pandharpur. The pilgrimage to Pandharpur from Āḷandi was re-started twice in a year – during the month of *Āśāḍa* and *Kārtik*. Saṅt Ekanāth recalled the last declaration of Māvuli that he had heard in the cave:

> *'May the path of Nivṛtti awaken the fervour for the name of Hari;*
> *All my doubts on action and path here and hereafter have dissolved;*
> *The four* puruṣārthas *– efforts, so also my social obligations;*
> *And the attractions for sense objects have merged in the name Rāma-Kṛṣṇa.*
> *In the benign shade of Kalpavṛkṣa all imagination vanished;*
> *After drinking the nectar of* bhakti *all my worries are dispelled;*
> *Name is absorbed in the mind to stay in Vaikunṭha;*
> *The three fevers, vices and all limitations vanished.*
> *The secret of all* Veda-Śāstras *has been revealed; I have recognised* Ātmārāma,
> *My dependency on the web of infatuation and desire has been destroyed.*
> *The pangs of separation of* buddhi *and* bodha *– awareness of many births have vanished;*
> *New energy is flowing in the limbs; the eye of the eye has opened the inner vision;*
> *There is divine transformation in body and nectar scattered*

all over;
The ten dimensions are Brahman and in full blossoms of wisdom.
Guru Nivṛtti's grace is ever on me and my blindness is cured and no-otherness *has dawned;*
Life got its purpose with the vision of ātmārāma *and the darkness of ignorance quelled;*
Nivṛttināth showered the Gaṅgā of jñāna on Jñānadev;
May His path prosper, let there be fervor for the name of Hari."[74]

During their lifetime, Paiṭhan had been instrumental in recognising the greatness of the Quartet – Nivṛttināth, Jñānadev, Sopāndev and Muktābāi. More than two centuries later, it was again given to Ekanāth, the saint of Paithan to resurrect Jñānadev as well as the Quartet, to revive the tradition of *bhakti* and in turn the Māṇus *Dharma*. Through his pilgrimage to the root, as he had called it, Saint Ekanāth realised his *no-otherness* with Jñānadev Māvuli, and became *immortal* in the heart of *bhakti* tradition.

□

74. धर्म जागो निवृत्तीचा हरि-नामें उत्साहो, कर्म धर्म लोपलें माझें फिटला सन्देहो। धर्म अर्थ काम पूर्ण दान मान समूहो, नेघ मी इंद्रिय-वृत्ति राम-कृष्ण-नाम टाहो।। १।। कल्पना मावळली कल्पवृक्ष-तळवटीं, चिंता हारपली माझी नित्य अमृताची वाटी। मन हे मग्न झालें नित्य वसे वैकुंठीं, ताप-त्रय पाप गेलें नाना दोषांचे थाटीं।। २।। आत्मा-राम निर्गमले वेद-शास्त्र-गुह्य-ज्ञानें, वासना चि मोहो-जाळी ते विराली नाना स्थानें। फुटले नाना घट तुटलीं बंधनें, सुटलिया जीव-ग्रंथी ऐसें केलें गुरु-ज्ञानें ।। ३।। बुद्धि बोध सवंगडे सजीव कर-चरण, नयनीं नयन झाले चक्षु मी समाधान। दिव्य देह अमृत-कळा दश दिशा परिघन, सर्व हें ब्रह्म झालें फळलें विज्ञान।। ४।। निवृत्ति गुरु माझा अंधपण फेडिलों, सर्वत्र दृष्टि झाली एक तत्त्वें राहिलों। निरसली माया-मोहो रामांजन लेइलों, ज्ञानदेवो ज्ञान-गन्गो निवृत्ती बुडविलों।। ५।।

The Pilgrimage (Epilogue)

'Sweet is your form, sweeter your name; always shower me with love for you.
Ever be my eyes on you; O resplendent companion of Rakhumāyī!
Only this boon is enough O Viṭṭhala and Mother; be ever in my heart.
Tukā says he does not seek anything else; all bliss is ever there at your feet.'[75]

Groups of pilgrims had started arriving at Āḷandi and the whole milieu was charged with feelings of brotherhood arising out of love for God in every being – the path of *bhakti*! The *abhaṅgs* were sung by different groups at the *samādhi* of Jñānadev Māvuli. Devavrit was swept away in a flood of emotions. The past ten days had been of greatest significance in his life. He had learnt to see the world and also life with a fresh perspective. He had understood that life offers opportunities for more than just survival; that it is the reason to share, to help and to love, and love unconditionally. It was really surprising that though he was a person with a

75. गोड तुझे रुप गोड तुझे नाम। देईं मज प्रेम सर्व काळ देईं प्रेम।। १।।
सदा माझे डोळे जडो तुझे मूर्ती। रखुमाईच्या पती सोयरिया।। २।।
विठु माउलिए हा चि वर देईं। संचरोनि राही हृदयी माझा।। ३।।
तुका म्हणे कांही न मांगो आणीक। तुझे पायीं सुख सर्व आहे।। ४।।

scientific temper, he had accepted the path of faith, though not willingly! He had found it hard to believe the infinite patience and forbearance of the children who were persecuted by the society. At such times when Devavrit's mind refused to believe, Viṣṇu Śāstriji pointed out that it had not only happened with the Quartet, but almost all the lovers of God; and that even in the present times we have such persons – not only lovers of God, but even the ordinary people who bear with such unjust treatment from the society. He said that maybe these people evoke jealousy in others, either through their inherent talents and skills, or through their purity and simplicity! Śāstriji had then reminded him that it was really not a question of patience or forbearance, but that of the art of absorbing the persecution and responding positively through infinite love and understanding, without a trace of pain or pity. This is the greatest contribution of the *bhakti* movement.

To illustrate, he had narrated an old parable: "Once while a king was strolling in the palace orchard, a stone hit him. The guards searched for the culprit and brought an old and famished beggar. The king noted that the beggar had no fear, but a mild curiosity. When asked by the minister the reason for pelting the stone, which had hurt the king, the beggar only looked at the ripe mangoes on the tree under which the king was, when the stone had hit him, and then at the king. The beggar had smiled and repeated the gesture! The king then commanded the minister to free the beggar and to feed him properly.

The minister after following the command asked the reason for this grand gesture of the king, who replied: "The tree gives fruits on being pelted with stones; the Earth bears food on plowing; the river gives pure water in spite of our polluting it; and Nature returns in abundance as a response to all the ill treatment meted out to it by man. I am a human being who is supposed to be on the top of creation. Added to this, I am a king. It is only just and right that I should respond to a hungry man with food. Moreover, the fruit or the food is not my creation. It is not even mine. I am just a caretaker who is supposed to look after the needs of my subjects. Should I not feed a hungry man of my kingdom who threw a stone at a tree for a fruit?"

He was sitting on the steps of the *ghāt* of Iṅdrāyaṇi, when he remembered the dialogues he had with Vishnuji. He had entertained the query we all have about *bhakti*: 'what is its most important aspect?'

Without hesitation Vishnuji had responded: 'Faith' and continued that it is faith which leads one to the point of surrender. Devavrit had reacted that it was difficult if not impossible for an educated person to have blind faith.

Vishnuji had only laughed at this remark and had clarified: "Devavrit, it is impossible to live even day-to-day life without faith and the beauty is that we all have it in abundance! We travel in a transport bus, having faith in the driver that he will take us safely to our destinations; we have faith in the doctor that he will cure us of our ailments; faith in the government, faith in one another, and the greatest faith in tomorrow! The difference between the faith in our daily transactions and *bhakti* is: we have faith in things and people, while a *bhakta* has *trust* – pure faith in this whole Existence, the driving force of the universe!"

He had paused for a while allowing this to sink in. Then he continued: "On observing life around, including our own, we realise that we all have this faith and so, start taking steps towards *trust* – a conviction that everything that happens in life is *His* play and we are but *His* instruments. Faith is like a child catching hold of the father's fingers, and trust is the feeling the child gets when the father catches hold of its hand!" Śāstriji's silence was full.

They were taking a walk one evening, climbing the small hillock that gave the overview of Āḷaṅdi. Devavrit felt extremely happy at the thought that they were walking on the same ground that would have been sanctified by the lotus feet of Māvuli! Devavrit exclaimed happily: "I think I understand

Śāstriji. Just now there was a flash – are we not treading on the same ground and perhaps even the same spots that were covered by Māvuli? That very thought is giving me so much joy! It had never crossed my mind to come to this sacred place. It all happened on its own!"

It was twilight and the sun was in the western horizon, Śāstriji stopped to behold the setting sun. Devavrit stopped totally, even his mind became silent and he felt himself merge with beauty and *the Existence*! On their way back, they had remained silent; more so, as Devavrit was holding on to his first experience of this kind!

He remembered, that trust of *bhakti* dawns when one stops *thinking* and starts *feeling*! For thinking engages one in trivia, while feeling expands the heart and one starts trusting this grand Existence for which, the word 'Māvuli' – 'mother' is used. She takes every being and thing in her bosom and nurtures them. Devavrit heard the bells from the temple announcing the evening *pūjā*. Getting up, he started walking. How things had changed his life in a small span of a few days! The questions pestering his mind had reduced remarkably and it appeared as though he had become simpler and trusting. With that, he became aware of daily and the so-called ordinary miracles happening in his life!

When he walked in the sun, the heat brought some drops of sweat, and just at that precise moment, a mild breeze blew giving a cool feeling; when his throat was parched, he felt as though Mother Iṅdrāyaṇi invited him for a drink. Such small needs were fulfilled without any effort on his part. His vision of the world changed as he started seeing beauty in every being and everything around him. It was then it dawned upon him that 'this has been so always, only my eyes were looking in a different direction!'

Discrimination between the so-called educated and the illiterate had vanished completely from his mind. On the contrary, he had started enjoying the company of simple folk. When he interacted with them, he realised that *trust* is natural to them. They had total *trust* that they were able to reach Āḷandi only because Māvuli had called them. Some of them had told him that in spite of wanting to come here, they had failed, not due to certain events forcing them to post-pone their journey, but because Māvuli had not called them! He had learnt to eat the simple food offered by them, and he in turn, happily shared his food with them. Another great fact was seen by him – they not only shared the food, but their feeling of oneness and the joy they felt with one another! It appeared the world had shrunk, or had his world expanded?

The world has no doubt developed and presently appears to have improved its standard of living by shrinking itself into a global village. But and this 'but' is extremely important: our hearts have not expanded proportionately, instead, our egotism – sense of 'I am doing' is expanding day-after-day! Consequently, there is stress in our thinking and strain in our actions! When these thoughts were passing through Devavrit's mind, his eyes fell on the steady flow of Iṅdrāyaṇi. To his pleasant surprise, it struck him that in there was another mandatory aspect in *bhakti*: *śaraṇāgati* – total surrender. It struck Devavrit suddenly, that before every thought, word and deed, Jñānadev Māvuli had either sought the permission of his *guru*, Nivṛttināth or took care to mention his name. This apparently small act had absolved him of the great impediment called *ahaṅkāra*. Aspiration to seek, inspiration to start the search and grit to continue this pilgrimage of the soul is ever governed and guided by the grace of *guru* if one is fortunate, else the grace of God for others. It is like water flowing from higher to the lower level, the *bhakta* has to be at a lower level for the grace to flow. And surrender is that mandatory act for receiving the grace!

Now Devavrit understood how *nāmasmaraṇam*—or the act of remembering God through chanting of name helped in developing faith which led the devotee to *śraddhā* - trust and finally *śaraṇāgati.* Chanting helps in channelising the mental energy, which can be done at any time and all the time, during any activity or rest! '*Jai Jai Rāmakṛṣṇa Hari*' or any other name can work wonders. There is however, only one catch: one has to regain one's innocence and simplicity! Devavrit had started regaining them in the company of simple village-folk. He had been directed to come to Āḷaṅdi by Satheji, an educated *vārkari*! He did not want to get involved further into thinking. Just then, he heard the bells of the temple resounding in the atmosphere. Looking at Iṅdrāyaṇi with loving reverence, he rose and started walking towards the temple.

Devavrit entered the temple where the fragrance of flowers and incense greeted him. He stood facing the sanctum sanctorum. Śāstriji was waving the *ārati* in front of the image of Lord Siddheśwar. All of them were singing the chorus '*Jai Jai Rāmakṛṣṇa Hari*' allowing the sound not only outside, but more so inside as if to awaken the inner being and to merge into the ever-present divinity all around! When Śāstriji approached him with the *ārati*, a strange ethereal smile adorned his lips, some sort of pride dancing in those gentle eyes. He had seen the same expression in his father when he had completed his education.

Devavrit bent down to touch the feet of his guide and *guru*. Śāstriji touched his back in blessing. In that touch, he received not only blessings but the key for opening the heart leading to a different kind of insight, full and brimming!

A little later, a *kīrtanbua* started singing an *abhaṅg* of Saint Tukārām:

> '*Though smaller than the smallest particle; Tukā is as vast as the sky!*
> *I discarded my interest for this physical body; as it is only a form in this temporal world.*
> *Dissociating from Tripuṭi*[76] *- the triad of experience; the lamp of wisdom was lit inside.*
> *Tukā says, now my life continues; only for fulfilling my*

---

76. *Tripuṭi* is the mandatory triad for any experience (perceived-perception-perceiver), knowledge (known-knowing-knower) or action (action-acting-actor).

obligation to others.'[77]

The mood, the occasion and the ambience were so relevant that Devavrit joined others in flowing with the singer and the listeners. It was so wonderful that there was total *being* in the ocean of *bhāva,* without any wall of *otherness.* While singing and chanting continued, Devavrit remained in the most coveted state he had been seeking all his life. And time as such, vanished from his mind!

A gentle tap on his shoulder brought him to the reality without. Turning in the direction, Devavrit saw Satheji, who had the same joy and pride in his eyes that he had beheld in Śāstriji.

"Shall we go on the pilgrimage?" Satheji asked Devavrit gently.

And Devavrit nodded in blissful affirmation!

□□□

77. अणुरणिया थोकडा। तुका आकाशा एवढा।। १।। गिळुन सांडिले कलेवर। भव भ्रमाचा आकार।। २।। सांडिली त्रिपुटी। दीप उजळला घटी।। ३।। तुका म्हणे आता। उरलो उपकारा पुरता।। ४।।